Josie's getting a makeover . . .
whether she wants it or not!

"What time is Red coming?" Cat asked Josie.

"About an hour," Josie replied. She became aware that Cat was looking at her strangely. "What are you staring at?"

"Your hair. Have you ever thought about cutting your bangs?"

Oh, sure," Josie said. "Sometimes I can't sleep at night thinking about it."

"Seriously," Cat went on, "let me see what I can do with your hair."

Josie clutched her head protectively. "No way you're coming near me with scissors."

"I won't cut it," Cat said. "I just want to try some of these hot curlers on it. Really, Josie, it'll be fun. I'll give you a whole new look."

Books in the THREE OF A KIND series
Available from HarperPaperbacks

Three of a KIND

Two's Company, Four's a Crowd

Marilyn Kaye

HarperPaperbacks
A Division of HarperCollinsPublishers

For Polly Winograd

HarperPaperbacks *A Division of* HarperCollins*Publishers*
10 East 53rd Street, New York, N.Y. 10022

Produced by Daniel Weiss Associates, Inc.
33 West 17th Street, New York, New York 10011.

RL 4.9   IL 008–013

First printing: March, 1991

Printed in the United States of America

HarperPaperbacks and colophon are trademarks of
HarperCollins*Publishers*

10 9 8 7 6 5 4 3 2 1

Two's Company,
Four's a Crowd

One

At noon on the first Friday in November, the cafeteria at Green Falls Junior High was in its usual state of noisy commotion. Cat Morgan picked up her lunch tray and started toward her table. Along the way, she was greeted by several classmates at other tables, and she paused to chat briefly with a few. Finally she reached the table where she'd been having lunch every weekday for the past two months.

"Hi, guys," she hailed her lunchmates.

"Hi," they chorused as Cat sat down.

"Your hair's different," Marla Eastman noticed. "What did you do, get a perm?"

"No," Cat replied, fingering a glossy black ringlet. "I just used hot curlers."

"How come?" Trisha Heller asked.

"I don't know. I felt like doing something different." She moved her head from side to side. "What do you think?"

Marla, Trisha, Sharon, Karen, and Britt all stopped eating and gave Cat's hair their full attention. Cat waited for them to pass judgment.

"It's cute," Britt stated.

"I like it," Sharon and Karen said simultaneously.

Marla wasn't so quick to approve. "It's okay, but I like it better straight."

Cat wasn't disturbed by her comment. Since Marla was her closest friend, Cat felt she was entitled to criticize. "You just want to be the only one with curly hair," she told Marla in a teasing voice. Marla ran a hand through her mass of dark curls and grinned.

"I wish I could change *my* hair," Trisha said. "Sometimes I'm sorry I had it cut so short. It always looks the same."

"Short hair suits you," Cat assured her.

"But don't you think it's kind of boring?" Trisha asked anxiously.

This set off one of their typical lunchtime discussions, arguing the merits of short hair versus long hair. As the conversation took its usual course, Cat's attention wandered and she began looking around the cafeteria.

Everything looked so familiar, as if she'd been coming here for all of her thirteen years. It was weird to think that only three months ago she'd been a total stranger, not just to this school, but to Green Falls, Vermont. Before that, she'd been Cat O'Grady of

Willoughby Hall, an orphan. Then Annie and Ben Morgan came into her life and everything changed. Now, here she was, adopted, with a new home, new parents, and a new name.

To top it all off, she'd become a recognized person at school, with very cool friends and a boyfriend who was co-captain of the football team. She had everything she'd ever wanted.

Unfortunately, there was something else that came with adoption. Sisters. Not content with getting one daughter, Annie and Ben had adopted two other thirteen-year-old girls, Cat's Willoughby Hall roommates. A sigh escaped her lips as she spotted one of them.

"What are you moaning about?" Marla demanded.

Cat responded simply, "Look at Josie."

Heads turned in the direction Cat indicated. Sharon, who was supposed to wear glasses but wouldn't because she was so vain, squinted. "Is she sitting with *boys*?"

Cat nodded sadly. It was an unwritten law at Green Falls Junior High that boys sat with boys in the cafeteria and girls sat with girls. Cat had figured that out the first week of school. It was okay to stop by a boy's table and talk, and the boys could do the same with the girls. But you never sat down with the opposite sex. Cat wasn't sure why, but that didn't matter. It was the way things were. Either Josie was so dense that she hadn't picked up on it, or she was intentionally disregarding the rules.

"Who are they?" Sharon asked. Her eyes became narrow slits as she tried to make out Josie's lunch companions.

Cat couldn't get a good look at the faces, but the boys were taller than the average junior high student. "Basketball players," she decided.

"That makes sense," Marla said. "She's on the team."

"The only girl on the boys' basketball team," Britt mused. "Doesn't that make her feel weird?"

"Are you kidding?" Cat snorted. "Sometimes Josie thinks she *is* a boy."

Karen giggled. "You know, from a distance she almost looks like one, with her short hair and those beat-up jeans."

"Not to mention the fact that she has no figure whatsoever," Cat added. "And she doesn't even care."

"Hi, Becka," Marla called out.

Cat turned to see her other sister coming toward their table.

"You want to join us?" Marla asked.

"No, thanks," the short, fair-haired girl replied. "I have to go to a newspaper staff meeting. Cat, did Mademoiselle Casalls hand back the French quizzes this morning?"

Cat nodded. "I got a B plus."

"Do you have her for French, too?" Trisha asked Becka.

Becka nodded. "Fifth period." She started chewing on a fingernail.

"Stop that," Cat scolded her. "And don't tell me you're worried about getting the quiz back." She turned to the others. "Becka's made A's on every French quiz this term. You can imagine how that makes *me* look."

"You could be making A's if you really wanted to," Becka pointed out.

Cat sniffed. "Yeah, if I had my very own private bedroom to study in." The fact that Becka had gotten the newly renovated bedroom at home still rankled her. Especially when *she* was still sharing a room with Josie, and there was no telling when Ben would get another bedroom done.

"That wouldn't help," Britt said. "I've got my own room and I'm still making B's."

"Hey, Cat, don't faint, but look who's coming," Becka said.

Cat looked up to see Todd Murphy and two other boys heading up the aisle. Becka batted her eyes and pretended to swoon. Cat made a face at her. Becka giggled and took off.

Cat rearranged her features and formed her special smile as Todd drew nearer. He responded with his appealing lopsided grin and paused at the table. "How ya doing?"

"Fine," Cat said. "How are you?" She tossed her

5

head so the new curls bobbed around her shoulders. Todd didn't seem to notice the new hairdo. Of course, she wasn't surprised. He never noticed things like that.

"Great," he said, shifting his weight from one foot to the other. One of the boys with him snickered.

"Uh, so I'll see ya later," Todd said hastily, and moved on with the boys.

Cat shook her head wearily as she gazed after his retreating figure. "What a great conversationalist."

"He doesn't need to be a good talker with eyes like that," Karen said. "Cat, you're so lucky."

Cat had to admit she was probably right. Todd was considered a great catch.

"What are you and Todd going to do this weekend?" Trisha asked.

Cat considered the question. "Well, it's Friday, right? That means there's a football game after school. First I'll watch Todd play, then we'll go over to my house for dinner. After that, we'll probably sit around and watch TV. On Saturday night we'll go to Luigi's for pizza, then to the movies. If we've already seen the movie, we'll go bowling. And then we'll go to Brownies for ice cream."

Marla raised her eyebrows. "Isn't that exactly what you did last weekend?"

Cat nodded. "And the weekend before that, and the weekend before that." She looked up at the clock. "I better get going. I have to stop at my locker. See you guys at the game."

She picked up her tray and headed to the conveyor belt. Just as she was putting her tray down, she felt someone come up alongside of her. She turned her head and met two eyes not quite as green as her own.

Her lips automatically formed a stiff, even smile. "Hello, Heather."

Heather Beaumont's face bore an identical expression. "Hello, Cat."

That was the extent of their conversation. Cat watched thoughtfully as Heather sauntered away, her long blond hair cascading down her shoulders. No one would ever in a million years call them friends, but at least now they were acting civil to each other.

Which was a definite improvement, considering their past relationship. It had started on registration day, when Heather had conned Cat into choosing the strictest teacher in school for English. Cat retaliated by flirting with Todd, who was Heather's numero uno back then. Heather tried to get back at her by setting up a public humiliation for Becka and arranging to keep Josie off the basketball team. Cat not only managed to rescue her sisters, she also got the ultimate revenge—snaring Todd.

By now, Heather must have realized that Cat Morgan was not to be pushed around. She was off the warpath. It was hard for Cat to believe Heather had actually given up, but if she'd wanted to get back at Cat, she would have pulled something by now. All had been peaceful between them lately.

Too peaceful. In the strangest way, Cat sort of missed the excitement of wondering when, where, and how Heather would strike next.

That's crazy, Cat told herself sternly. *Everything's perfect. You're pretty and popular, and you haven't a care in the world.*

Then why did she feel so . . . so *blah*?

Becka tried very hard not to daydream in French class. She couldn't afford to, since Mademoiselle Casalls always seemed to know when someone's attention was drifting away. Besides, Becka was enchanted by the teacher's voice, with its beautiful, exotic accent.

She was fun to watch, too. Her face was expressive, and as she talked she used her hands a lot, making dramatic gestures to emphasize what she was saying. And her clothes were very stylish. Cat was always talking about how chic Mademoiselle Casalls was. It was one of the few subjects she and Becka agreed on.

Gazing at the teacher now, Becka admired her look. Maybe someday *she'd* wear a short black skirt and a white silk blouse, with a bright red scarf at the neck and huge gold hoop earrings. She tried to envision herself looking as sophisticated as her teacher, with long red nails and lips the exact same color. But try as she might, all she saw in her mind was a short, frizzy-haired, slightly chunky thirteen-year-old with chewed fingernails.

"Becka!"

Becka's vision cleared. "*Oui*, mademoiselle?"

"Please, *s'il vous plâit*, I must have your full attention!"

She spoke kindly, with a smile, but Becka flushed. From the seat in front of her, her friend Patty turned and winked in sympathy.

"Now, class," the teacher continued, "I shall distribute your examinations. Some of you did very well, and I am pleased." Then the corners of her mouth turned down. "But most of you . . . *ooh la la*, you must begin to study!"

She began passing out the papers. Becka automatically began chewing on her thumbnail. At this rate, she'd never have nails like Mademoiselle Casalls.

The teacher stood before her. Her blue eyes warmed as she presented the paper to Becka. "*Très bien,* Becka! Very good." To the class, she announced, "Becka had the only score which was perfect!"

Once again, Becka flushed, but this time with pleasure. She sensed, rather than saw, the admiring glances from some of her classmates. Of course, there was probably a hostile look from one or two, but that didn't bother her. Her friend Patty turned again and gave her a thumbs-up sign.

The bell rang, and everyone began gathering up their books. "What a relief," Patty told Becka. "I only missed two."

"I can't believe I got all those conjugations," Becka said. "Are you going to the game after school?"

9

"Yeah," Patty replied. "Meet me and Lisa at my locker, and we'll sit together, okay?" They headed for the door. A boy stood there, looking at his paper with a rueful expression. He was blocking their way.

"Excuse me," Becka murmured.

He looked up. "Sorry," he said and stepped aside. He indicated his test paper. "I really blew this one."

"I gotta run," Patty said. She took off down the hall. But there was something about the boy's deep brown eyes that held Becka there in the doorway.

"It was harder than usual," she said.

He grinned. "But not for you, right?" Pulling her paper out from between her notebooks, he whistled. "You must really study this stuff."

He's cute, Becka thought. *But he probably thinks I'm some boring brainy type who buries herself in books.* "Not *that* much," she said.

He grinned. "Okay, I guess maybe you're just a natural genius. Check this out." He held up his own paper and hung his head in mock shame.

Trying not to appear shocked by the big red D on the paper, Becka said, "Gee, I'm sorry."

He shrugged. "It's not your fault. I'm just a lazy bum." His eyes were dancing.

"I'm sure that's not true," Becka said quickly. "I mean, some subjects come easier to some people than to others."

"Right," he said. "That's life."

Becka repeated his words in French. *"C'est la vie."*

10

He laughed. "See? You *are* a genius!" With a wave, he took off.

Becka's skin was tingling and her heart was pounding as she walked in the opposite direction. Her mind raced through the roll call until she reached his name. Keith Doyle.

He had the nicest smile. . . .

The entire crowd in the bleachers stood up, and a deafening roar filled the air. Cat rose with the others and assumed the noise meant that Green Falls had won the game. She'd spent the past half hour filing her nails.

Out on the field, the players were slapping each other on the back and heading over to the door leading to the gym. The cheerleaders, led by Heather, went into a final chorus of "Green Falls Forever," and people began moving out of the bleachers.

"How did Todd do?" Cat asked Britt.

Britt looked at her in surprise. "Didn't you see? He scored two touchdowns!"

"Isn't that what he scored last week?" Cat asked. "I think he's in a rut."

When they reached the bottom of the bleachers, Cat turned to her friends. "Where are you guys going?"

"Back to my house," Marla said. "My sister said maybe she'd take us all to Dream Burger."

Cat eyed them enviously. She'd always wanted to go to Dream Burger. It was the major high school

11

hangout in Green Falls, and no junior high student dared go there without being accompanied by a high school student. "Lucky you," she said.

"Lucky *us?*" Trisha's eyebrows shot up. "*You're* the one with a real live date!"

"Yeah, I guess," Cat said. She waved good-bye to her friends and pulled her jacket tighter against the brisk autumn wind.

"Great game, huh?" Josie stood there, her hands deep in the pockets of her windbreaker.

"Was it?" Cat asked vaguely.

"Weren't you watching?"

"Yeah, sure."

Josie looked at her reprovingly. "Your boyfriend's co-captain, Cat. The least you could do is try to understand the game."

Cat made a "Who cares?" gesture. "Josie, if you knew anything about boys, you'd realize that it doesn't matter if you understand football or not."

Becka joined them. "You guys going home?"

"I have to wait for Todd," Cat said. "He's coming over for dinner."

"So's Red," Josie said.

"That's nice," Becka said, but something in her face caught Cat's eye.

"What's your problem?"

"Nothing . . . it's just that, well, you've got Todd, and Josie's got Red—"

"Wait a minute," Josie interrupted. "There's a big

difference. Red's a friend, not a date. I mean, he lives next door, for crying out loud."

"The boy next door," Becka repeated. "That's the name of a romance book I read." Her eyes shifted away from Josie's face and seemed to focus on something beyond her.

"Well, there's nothing romantic about me and Red MacPherson," Josie retorted. "So don't start drumming up one of your usual fantasies. I better go find him. See you at home."

"She's always saying that about Red," Cat noted. "Personally, I think it's bull. I mean, why would she hang around with him all the time if she wasn't feeling at least a tiny bit romantic about him?"

Becka didn't respond. She was distracted by a group of passing boys. One of them wore a baseball cap, and he tipped it as he passed. "*Bonjour*, mademoiselle!"

Becka giggled. "It's too late for *bonjour*," she called after him. "*Bonsoir*, monsieur!"

"How do you know Keith Doyle?" Cat asked.

"He's in my French class. Don't you think he's cute?"

"Very. Well, I guess I ought to go meet Todd."

"Mmm." Becka was still staring after Keith Doyle.

As she walked over to the gym entrance, Cat wondered if she had time to run into the building and fix her hair and makeup. She decided it wasn't worth the effort. Todd wouldn't even notice.

Behind her, she heard two people talking in

French. She turned and saw Mademoiselle Casalls with a man. "*Bonjour*, mademoiselle," she said, and then remembered Becka's words to Keith Doyle. "I mean, *bonsoir*."

"*Bonsoir*, Catherine," the French teacher replied. She introduced Cat to the man by her side. "This is my very good friend Monsieur Christophe Durand, who is visiting from Paris."

He murmured something that sounded like "enchanted."

"How do you do?" Cat said politely. Meanwhile, she was thinking that this Monsieur Durand had to be the handsomest man she'd ever seen. He looked like a movie star. And he wasn't just good-looking. Even in casual jeans, he had style. She loved the way he had a sweater tied around his shoulders.

"My, it is getting cold," Mademoiselle Casalls murmured. Her friend whipped off his sweater and placed it around her shoulders. "*Merci, mon cheri,*" she murmured. "*Au revoir*, Catherine."

"*Au revoir,*" Cat echoed. With appreciation, she watched the couple walk away. It was so romantic how he had his hand lightly on her arm, like a real escort.

"Hiya, babe." Todd stood there, his freshly washed hair hanging over his forehead in wet clumps.

Cat tore her eyes away from the French couple and smiled at Todd. "Hi. Congratulations. That was a great game."

Todd nodded. "Yeah, wild, huh? Did you see Erickson make that pass in the third quarter?"

They started off toward the Morgan home, and Todd began a play-by-play description of the game. As he talked, Cat smiled and nodded and occasionally gasped. Every once in a while she said, "Really?" and "Oh, wow," and "You're kidding!" In the past few weeks, it had become a routine. Todd talked sports, and Cat pretended to listen. She used the time to mentally put together her outfits for the next school week.

Finally, they reached the big old farmhouse the Morgans called home. Every time she walked up the driveway, Cat recalled her dismay the first time she saw the place. It had looked like a rundown dump to her. But a month ago, Ben had finally fixed the lopsided shutters and the sagging porch. Now, it looked like—well, still a little rundown, but it looked like home.

Todd was still rambling on about the game as they climbed the steps, automatically avoiding the one that creaked. Annie appeared at the door. "Hi, we were wondering about you guys! Come on in, dinner's on the table."

"Great," Todd said. "I'm starving. I think I could eat a horse."

Cat grimaced. That was what he *always* said.

But the sight of the dinner table cheered her. Josie had been giving Annie cooking lessons, and they were beginning to pay off. Plus, she had to admit

15

there was something nice about seeing the whole family gathered around the table in the cozy dining room. The setting sun peeking through the windows bathed the room in a golden light. Remembering her years sitting with a bunch of screeching orphans at long tables in a huge, ugly dining hall, Cat found herself smiling happily as she kissed Ben on the cheek and took her seat.

The platters of chicken, roast potatoes, and green beans began making the rounds. "How was the game?" Ben asked Todd.

Cat closed her eyes and stifled a groan. That was the wrong question. Now she'd have to listen—or not listen—to the whole story all over again. And with Ben, Annie, Red, and Josie urging Todd on and showing actual interest, Todd went into even more detail.

Tuning him out, Cat concentrated on her food. As she ate, her eyes roamed the table. Annie and Ben . . . even though they'd been married for at least fifteen years, they still seemed to love each other. Cat wondered how they were able to make a relationship last so long. Probably because they had so much in common, she decided. Like fixing up this old house, the health-food store across the street, their daughters.

She looked at Josie and Red, both of whom were bombarding Todd with questions about the game. They had a lot in common, too. Red hair, for one thing. Also they were practical, they didn't care about clothes or social things, and they were both seriously into sports and horses.

Her eyes shifted to Becka. Becka's head was down as she ate, and Cat suspected there was a book on her lap, hidden by the tablecloth. Someday, Cat mused, Becka would meet a boy she had stuff in common with, and . . . they'd read to each other or something.

Then she looked at Todd. His face was animated as he described how he'd tackled some guy on the other team. His true-blue eyes were gleaming like sapphires, and his hair, now dry, hung like silk down his forehead. He was awfully good-looking.

The girls at school were right, Cat assured herself. She *was* lucky.

She poked at her green beans and considered Mademoiselle Casalls and her French boyfriend. What were they doing right now? Probably sitting in some fancy restaurant, the kind with candles and flowers on the table and soft music in the background. Maybe, right now, they were gazing deeply into each other's eyes and clinking their glasses of champagne.

What would they be talking about? Cat didn't have the faintest idea. But she had a pretty good feeling it wasn't football.

Two

Saturday mornings were the only really busy times in Morgan's Country Foods, and this week was no exception. For three hours, Cat had been behind the checkout counter ringing up purchases. Annie ran from one customer to another, while Ben hastily scrawled prices on cards to put up in front of the fruit bins. Becka was scurrying around, gathering items in a basket for a phone-in order.

"Becka, please put this by the apples," Ben called, waving a price sign in the air.

At the same time, Annie's voice rang out. "Becka, could you check in the back for strawberry jam?"

Becka plunked the basket down on the checkout counter. "I've only got two hands," she muttered before heading to the back of the store.

Cat had to grin. Back when they'd first arrived at

18

the Morgans', Becka had been Little Miss Perfect, working like a maniac and never complaining. Now that she was comfortable and secure in her new home, she could whine like a normal teenager.

"That will be four seventy-five," Cat told the waiting customer. She took the woman's money, gave her some change, and handed over a bag of purchases.

There was a momentary lull in activity at the checkout counter. Cat had just plunked her elbows on the counter and rested her chin in her hands when the telephone rang. With a weary sigh, she reached for it. "Morgan's Country Foods."

"Cat, hi, it's Marla."

Cat brightened. The girls weren't supposed to use the store phone for social visits, but both Annie and Ben were occupied, so she relaxed. "Hi. What's up? Did you guys go to Dream Burger last night?"

"No, my sister had a last-minute date and finked out on us. But that's why I'm calling. She says she'll take me there for lunch in about fifteen minutes. Want to come?"

"I'd love to!" Cat exclaimed. She lowered her voice as two more customers walked in. "I don't know how I'm going to get out of here, though. But I'll think of something."

"Great. Meet us in front of Dream Burger at one."

Hanging up the phone, Cat looked around. Josie was still at basketball practice. It had gotten fairly quiet in the store, but that probably wouldn't last. She knew it wouldn't be very nice to leave them all in the lurch, but how many chances did she get to go to Dream Burger? She resumed her position of elbows on counter, her chin in her hands.

Annie joined her at the counter. "Whew, what a morning. What time is it?"

"Quarter to one," Cat replied automatically.

Annie eyed her curiously. "Why so glum?"

Cat searched her mind for a good reason to leave the store. For once, her mental grab bag of excuses was empty. She couldn't think of even one acceptable story.

She gave up. "Marla's invited me to go to Dream Burger with her and her sister. In fifteen minutes."

Annie nodded. "Well, Josie should be back from practice in a few minutes, and you've been working awfully hard. I think you deserve a break."

Cat gazed at her in disbelief. "You mean, I can go?"

"Of course. Have a good time."

Amazing, Cat thought as she raced out of the store. Sometimes honesty really *was* the best policy.

There was just enough time to go home, pull a brush through her hair, apply some lipstick, and grab her pocketbook before heading down the road to Main Street.

She'd just arrived when she spotted Marla and her sister coming from the opposite direction. She'd met Chris before, briefly, at Marla's house. If Marla was pretty, Chris was gorgeous, with an incredible figure and masses of lustrous black curls streaming down her back.

Marla's eyes were sparkling with anticipation, and Cat tried not to show she was just as excited. "It's nice of you to take us here," she told Chris.

"No problem," Chris said easily. "Though why you two get such a kick out of going to a dive like this is beyond me." Behind her back, Cat and Marla rolled their eyes at each other. Maybe to *her* it was a dive. She could come here anytime she wanted.

Once inside, however, Cat had to admit that the place did look like—well, maybe not a dive, but not like anything special. It could be any burger joint in the world. There was a long counter with stools, and the rest of the small room was taken up with tiny, not-very-clean tables and beat-up chairs with cracked vinyl seats.

But the occupants of the seats made the place special—tall, good-looking guys, girls with great hair and an air of confidence. For a split second, Cat experienced a sensation totally unfamiliar to her—insecurity.

Marla read her mind. "We look just as good as these girls," she whispered staunchly. Trying to be objective, Cat scrutinized some of the girls. She decided Marla was right. They both looked older than thirteen, and they were just as pretty.

They followed Chris to a table. Once they sat down, Cat reached for the plastic-coated menu, but a look from Chris froze her hand in midair. "Don't bother with that," the older girl instructed her. "Just order a cheeseburger and fries. That's what everyone gets. They're always out of everything else anyway."

Cat was grateful for the tip. What if she had ordered a BLT and made a total fool of herself?

"Check out those guys," Marla hissed, cocking her head to the left.

Cat peered out of the corner of her eye. There were four of them, all blond, all big, and all with football jackets slung over their chairs. They had something else in common, too.

"They're all gorgeous," Cat breathed.

Chris waved to a girl who had just walked in. "Debbie! Over here."

"Hi, Chris." The girl slid into the fourth seat at their table. Chris introduced her to Marla and Cat, and the two of them started talking, pretty much ignoring the younger girls. Cat and Marla didn't care. It was enough just to be there and get a taste of what life would offer them in a couple of years. They gave their orders to a waitress and settled back to look around.

"I think we could pass for high school girls," Marla mused.

"It's the boys who are really different," Cat said. "They look so mature."

"Not like the guys we know." Marla sighed.

Cat agreed. She visualized the scene at Green Falls Junior High. Suddenly, every boy she knew seemed scrawny and awkward.

22

"Doesn't that guy over there look exactly like Tom Cruise?" Marla asked.

Cat took a look. For a moment she could have sworn he smiled at her. Wishful thinking, probably.

Beside them, Chris's voice rose slightly. "Are you serious? You're going to Escapade?"

"Shh," Debbie admonished her. "I said maybe."

"What's Escapade?" Cat asked.

"Nothing you need to know about," Debbie said shortly.

Chris was more forthcoming. "It's a new dance club, on Green Street."

"I've heard of it," Marla said. She looked at Debbie oddly. "Don't you have to be twenty-one to get into a place like that?"

"Well, there are rumors going around that they let anyone in," Chris explained.

"Oh, Marla," Cat said suddenly. "Turn very slowly to your right and look at the boy sitting at the counter. Third stool from the end."

Marla turned. "Wow."

That was an understatement. The tall, slender boy had fashionably longish black hair and one pierced ear. He wore a black turtleneck sweater and black jeans, and he looked like he could be a rock star.

He turned his head in their direction. Both girls quickly averted their eyes.

"He was looking at you," Marla said excitedly.

"No, at you," Cat returned. But she thought Marla was probably right.

Their food came and they all started eating. Cat thought the hamburger was tasteless and the french fries were greasy, but she didn't mind. Who cared about food when there were all these wonderful boys around?

Marla was barely touching her food, too, and her thoughts were obviously running along the same lines. "So many cute guys," she murmured.

"Don't get any bright ideas," her sister warned. "High school boys don't go out with junior high girls."

Cat nodded sadly. "We'll just have to wait," she told Marla.

"But we still have another year after this one," Marla mourned.

All too soon they finished, and Chris announced it was time to leave. At the door, Marla turned and gave the place one last, longing look. "Someday . . ."

"Yeah," Cat said. But someday seemed so far away. They opened the door and walked out. Just as Cat emerged, she saw Heather Beaumont and one of her awful friends, Blair Chase, crossing the pavement in front of them.

"What a nice day," Cat said loudly.

At the sound of her voice, Heather turned. She didn't say anything, but her eyes widened. Then she moved on.

Marla nudged Cat. "Perfect!"

Cat beamed. It was like frosting on a cake, having Heather see her come out of Dream Burger. Maybe she'd think Cat had been meeting a boy there. If only that were true . . .

Late that afternoon, Becka and her friend Lisa Simon left Jason Wister's house together.

"Honestly," Lisa grumbled, shaking her head. "Can you believe we had to have a newspaper staff meeting on *Saturday*? Couldn't we have waited until Monday after school?"

Becka smiled, but privately she didn't mind giving up a Saturday for the newspaper. Being on the staff was a lot of fun. She remembered how lonely she'd been two months ago, how hard it had been to make friends at school.

"Well, you know how Jason is," she reminded Lisa. "Being editor, he thinks everything's an emergency. He wanted to get that editorial in the next issue, which meant he had to have our approval today."

"Yeah, but why was he in such a rush?" Lisa asked. "I mean, what's the big deal about having an honor code?"

Becka felt she had to defend Jason. "He's afraid people are cheating, so he thinks all the students should sign an honor code, like the one they have at the high school."

Lisa sniffed. "No one *I* know cheats. And if people really did want to cheat, signing an honor code wouldn't stop them."

She had a point. There was something else about

Jason's honor code idea that bothered Becka. "What did you think of that part about having to turn people in if you see them cheating?"

Lisa wrinkled her nose. "I didn't like it. It's none of my business if someone cheats. Besides, I'd hate being a tattletale."

"Me, too," Becka agreed. "But I guess Jason thinks we have to protect the reputation of the school." She changed the subject. "Lisa, are you going to the dance?"

Lisa nodded. "You know Bobby Raines in our homeroom? He asked me."

"You're kidding! I've never even seen you two talking to each other."

"We never have," Lisa said. "I guess he's been admiring me from afar." She made a dramatic gesture, and Becka started giggling. Lisa was one of her favorite people. She sat next to Becka in homeroom, but it had taken Becka two weeks to get up the nerve to speak to her. Then it was no time at all before they became pals.

They were passing a playground where some boys were playing basketball. Becka stopped abruptly. "Isn't that Keith Doyle?"

Lisa looked. "Yeah. Why?"

Becka hesitated. Lisa was a good friend, though, and she was dying to confess. "I think he's so cute."

Lisa grinned. "Ah-ha! Well, you're absolutely right. He's very cute."

They watched the boys play. Keith had the ball,

while another boy guarded him, trying to prevent him from throwing it to the guy standing by the hoop. Keith shot the ball over the guard's head. It was high, and the boy by the hoop ran backward to catch it. It happened so fast, Becka didn't have time to jump out of the way before the boy slammed into her. And suddenly, she was sitting on the ground.

"Hey, I'm sorry!" the boy said.

Too stunned to move, Becka just sat there. Then Keith appeared. "You okay?"

I must look like an idiot, Becka thought in dismay. She started pulling herself up. Keith grabbed her hand and helped her.

"I'm fine," Becka said.

Keith dazzled her with his smile. "Are you sure?"

"Really, I'm okay," Becka insisted. *"Très bien, merci."*

Keith laughed. "It's Saturday. You can speak English."

"Hey, where's the ball?" called one of the boys still on the court. With a wink and a wave, Keith ran back to join them.

Becka looked at the hand Keith had held when he helped her up.

"I bet you're never going to wash that hand again," Lisa teased.

Becka laughed. "Very funny." Even so, she could almost feel his hand still there.

* * *

27

Josie sat cross-legged on her bed and studied the diagram Coach Meadows had passed out during practice that afternoon. It was a new play, a tricky one, but if the team could pull it off it would be brilliant. And she had a key part to play.

It was scary but exciting. Being the first girl on what had been an all-boys team was such a responsibility. The guys seemed to have accepted her, but she still felt like she had to prove herself worthy. By the time the first game rolled around next month, she wanted to be able to hold her own, to show them she was every bit as good as they were.

Staring at the diagram, she tried to commit it to memory. But she was distracted by a cry of distress coming from the direction of the closet.

"What's the matter?" Josie asked Cat.

Cat whirled around to face her. Her face was a picture of tragedy. "I don't have anything to wear tonight."

"Go naked," Josie suggested.

"Ha ha." Cat pointed a finger at the closet. "There's absolutely nothing in there."

"Gee, that's strange," Josie commented. "From here, I can see skirts and dresses and shirts. . . . I must be having hallucinations."

Cat threw up her hands in disgust. "What would you know? You haven't been out of those jeans in three months."

"That's not true," Josie objected. "I take them off every night before I go to bed."

28

Cat took one more look into the closet. "There's not one thing in here that Todd hasn't already seen."

"What does that matter?" Josie asked. "You're always saying he never notices what you wear anyway."

Cat crossed the room to her bed and flopped down. "That's the truth."

Josie glanced at her curiously. Ever since she'd returned from Dream Burger, Cat had been in the strangest mood, grumpy and sullen. That was the way she used to act all the time back at Willoughby Hall. But in the past few months, Josie had become accustomed to a slightly less obnoxious Cat. She hoped Cat wasn't returning to her old ways.

Becka walked in. "Hi."

"Who invited you in here?" Cat asked.

Becka appeared somewhat taken aback by her tone.

"Don't mind her," Josie said. "She's been growling all evening."

"How come?" Becka asked. "Did you have a fight with Todd?"

Cat got up and moved around the room restlessly. "No." She frowned as Becka sat down on her bed. "What do you think you're doing?"

"Sitting on your bed," Becka replied.

"What's the matter with yours?"

Becka gave her an abashed smile. "It gets lonely in there sometimes."

Cat brightened slightly. "Want to trade?"

"No." Turning to Josie, Becka asked, "Are you doing anything tonight?"

"Red's coming over. He's having some trouble with the algebra homework, and I'm going to help him."

"Oh my, that's so romantic," Cat sneered.

Josie and Becka exchanged puzzled looks. After years of living together, they were accustomed to Cat's moods. But she was usually cheerful on Saturday nights, especially since she'd started dating Todd.

"Cat, do you know Keith Doyle very well?" Becka asked.

"Not really. I've seen him at some parties. Why?"

"I was just wondering . . ."

"Keith Doyle," Josie said. "I've seen that name somewhere."

Cat was staring at Becka. Then comprehension filled her eyes. "Oh, I get it. You've got a crush on Keith Doyle."

Becka squirmed. "It's not a crush, exactly."

"Don't give me that," Cat said. "It's written all over your face. Is he interested in you?"

"I don't know. How can you tell if someone's interested in you?"

"Oh, you can tell," Cat said wisely. "The first time I met Todd, I knew. Of course, that's not enough. You have to work on a guy for a while to make him realize he likes you."

"Why?" Josie asked.

"Because these boys are very immature. They don't know what they want."

"You think Todd's immature?" Becka asked. "He's the same age you are."

"Girls mature faster than boys, everyone knows that," Cat told her. "We should really be going out with boys two or three years older than us."

"You're nuts," Josie stated. "What sixteen-year-old boy would want to go out with a thirteen-year-old girl?"

An expression of overwhelming sadness crossed Cat's face. "I know."

"I'll never understand it," Becka sighed. "I'm going downstairs." She pulled herself off the bed and left the room.

"What time is Red coming?" Cat asked Josie.

"About an hour," Josie replied. She became aware that Cat was looking at her strangely. "What are you staring at?"

"Your hair. Have you ever thought about cutting your bangs?"

"Oh, sure," Josie said. "Sometimes I can't sleep at night thinking about it."

"Seriously," Cat went on, "let me see what I can do with your hair."

Josie clutched her head protectively. "No way you're coming near me with scissors."

"I won't cut it," Cat said. "I just want to try some of these hot curlers on it. Really, Josie, it'll be fun. I'll give you a whole new look."

31

"But I'm perfectly happy with my old look," Josie protested.

"Come on," Cat wheedled. "Don't you want to look special for Red?"

Josie groaned in exasperation. "How many times do I have to tell you, I'm not interested in Red that way."

"Okay, okay," Cat said hastily. "Let me do it anyway. Please? It'll be fun to do something different."

Josie was totally bewildered by her pleading tone. For the first time that evening, Cat wasn't pouting or whining. Josie took pity on her.

"Okay," she relented. "But nothing too drastic."

For the next twenty minutes, Josie sat there obediently while Cat fussed over her. In horror, she gaped at the array of cosmetics Cat spread out on the dresser. She flinched as Cat tugged at her hair and wound her red locks around the hot curlers. But she kept her mouth shut. Cat was humming and looking almost excited as she applied some greasy slime to Josie's face.

When she finished, Josie felt like she'd been covered with plaster. "Cover your eyes," Cat commanded. Then she sprayed what felt like a quart of hair spray on Josie's hair. "Now, look at yourself!"

In shock, Josie stood before the mirror. Somehow, she forced her lips into something like a smile. "Nice," she lied. Actually, she thought she bore a close resemblance to a circus clown.

"Red's going to flip!" Cat exclaimed.

He sure will. But not in the way you think. Cat can be so thick, Josie thought. "We're just studying together, not going to a ball."

Cat disregarded that. "It doesn't matter. Come on, let's go show Annie and Ben."

With a silent sigh, Josie allowed herself to be dragged from their room and down the stairs. In the living room, Annie, Ben, and Becka were setting up a game of Scrabble. "Recognize this person?" Cat asked, thrusting Josie forward.

Josie wasn't surprised when they all stared at her, speechless.

"Josie, what did you do to yourself?" Ben asked.

Josie gave them a thin smile. With all the junk on her lips, she couldn't manage any more than that. "Ask Cat."

"Doesn't she look good?" Cat asked.

Annie was the first to recover. "Very nice. It's certainly a new look for you, Josie."

"And a major improvement," Cat added.

"I don't know about that," Ben said. "None of you girls need all that makeup to be beautiful."

"Oh, Ben," Cat teased. "You're a guy. You don't understand these things." She eyed Josie. "I think she looks fantastic."

She seemed so proud of her work that Josie had to say something. "Yeah, I feel really . . ." She struggled for an appropriate word. "Really beautiful. Thanks, Cat."

Cat beamed. Annie's eyes darted back and forth

33

between Josie and Cat in amusement. Ben still looked totally bewildered.

"I never thought you were interested in that sort of stuff," he finally said.

"Well, everyone likes a change now and then," Josie said lamely. "But this is just for today," she added hastily, before Cat could get any ideas.

Becka spoke up tentatively. "Isn't that a lot of green eye shadow?"

"I think it could be toned down a bit," Annie suggested gently.

Josie nodded. "Absolutely. I'll go take some of it off right now."

"No, no," Cat said. "It just needs some blending. And then we'll pick out something for you to wear."

This was going too far. "Uh-uh. I'm not getting dressed up to do algebra problems."

"Algebra," Annie echoed, and smiled. She turned to Ben. "Remember that?"

"Do I ever," Ben sighed. "My worst subject in high school," he told the girls.

"It had its benefits, though," Annie said, still smiling at him. Ben smiled back.

"You're right. It certainly did."

"What do you mean?" Becka asked.

"That's how Ben and I met," Annie explained. "I put an ad in the school newspaper offering to tutor people in algebra. Ben was my first customer."

Cat poked Josie in the ribs. Josie groaned and fell

back on the sofa. Once Cat got a notion in her head, it took nothing short of dynamite to blast it out.

"When is Todd coming for you?" Ben asked Cat.

Cat looked at the clock on the mantel. "Fifteen minutes. Guess I'd better get ready." She left the room.

"That's strange," Annie said. "Doesn't Cat usually spend at least an hour getting ready for a date with Todd?"

"Closer to two," Ben replied.

"I just hope he's on time and gets her out of the house fast," Josie said.

"Why?" Annie asked.

Josie grinned. "So I can get this stuff off my face before Red gets here."

Three

On Wednesday afternoon, Cat left her last class of the day and headed to her locker. Along the way, she stopped to watch Larry Jacobs, the student body president, tack a poster on the wall. A small crowd gathered around him.

"SAVE THE ENVIRONMENT," someone read out loud from the sign.

Those weren't the words that had caught Cat's eye. She focused on the next line: BENEFIT DANCE.

"What's this all about?" a girl asked Larry.

"The student council wants to start a recycling program here at school," he explained. "We're having the dance to raise money."

Cat had only the vaguest notion what a recycling program was, but if it was an excuse for a dance, it had to be something good.

36

Marla came up beside her. "The first dance of the school year," she noted. "I hope I can drum up a date with someone halfway decent."

"What about Bobby Kent?" Cat asked. "Hasn't he been hanging around you a lot lately?"

"I'm keeping my fingers crossed," Marla replied. "At least *you* know you don't have to worry about a date."

"Yeah," Cat said. Marla didn't pick up on the lack of enthusiasm in that word.

"It must be such a good feeling to know you've got a guy you can count on," Marla continued.

"Yeah," Cat said again. This time Marla noticed her tone.

"What's the matter?" Marla asked. "You sound like you're really down."

Cat shook her head. How could she describe these strange feelings of dissatisfaction? "It's nothing." She nodded toward the books in her arms. "Just tons of homework. Annie and Ben have been on me lately to get my grades up. I better go home and get started."

Clearly Marla wasn't entirely satisfied with that explanation. "Is everything okay between you and Todd?"

"Sure," Cat replied. "Nothing's changed." *Nothing ever changes,* she added silently.

Walking home, she thought about the upcoming dance. Maybe she could talk Ben and Annie into a new dress. It was a pretty good possibility. Why didn't the thought excite her more?

Her thoughts went back to a movie she'd seen recently. It was about a senior prom at a high school. The girls had worn long gowns and corsages, the boys tuxedos. The boys had been such gentlemen, too, helping the girls take their coats off and pulling out chairs for them. She knew the Green Falls Junior High dance wouldn't be like that. She couldn't even picture Todd in a tuxedo. As for manners, Todd was more likely to pull a chair out from *under* her.

That's not fair, she scolded herself. Todd had never done anything like that to her. But he could be so juvenile sometimes. She recalled the scene at Brownies Saturday night. A bunch of kids from school had been there. The boys had started blowing the wrappers off their straws, trying to see who could shoot their paper the farthest. Todd had really gotten into it. She couldn't imagine anything like that going on at Dream Burger.

By the time she got home, she'd worked herself into a thoroughly bad mood. The silence of the empty house didn't do much to improve her spirits. She dropped her books on the little table in the foyer where the mail was piled and went into the kitchen. Nothing in there interested her. Through the window, she saw that the door was open in the old shed. That meant Annie was painting. She went outside and walked across the yard.

"Hi," she said, entering the shed.

Annie stood before an easel. "Hi, honey." Her greeting was warm but preoccupied.

38

Cat moved around to look at the canvas on the easel. "That looks nice."

"I can't get the color right," Annie murmured.

When Annie was absorbed in a painting, she didn't see or hear anything around her. Of course, Cat knew that all she had to do was tell Annie she felt down, and she'd get all the attention she could handle. But nobody could help her with the way she was feeling, so why bother?

"I guess I'll go do homework," Cat said.

Even that extraordinary suggestion didn't distract Annie. But as Cat was walking out, Annie did look up. "Cat, there's a letter for you. On the table by the door."

"A letter? For me?"

"Mmm." Annie was dabbing paint on the canvas and frowning. Cat left and walked quickly back to the house. Who could be writing to her? She never got letters.

She went to the foyer and flipped through the mail on the little table. There it was, a plain white envelope with her name and address typed on it. There was no return address. She tore the envelope open and pulled out a white sheet of paper.

She read the letter quickly. Then she read it again. She was aware that her pulse had quickened.

The front door opened. "Hi," Becka said. "What's up?"

"Nothing." Cat stuffed the letter in her pocket, gathered her books, and ran upstairs where she could read it again in privacy. Once in her room, she smoothed the letter out on her bed. Then she reread it, slowly this time, savoring each and every word.

Dear Cat,

You don't know me, and I may never know you. But I saw you at Dream Burger on Saturday, and I can't get you out of my mind.

Do you believe in love at first sight? I didn't, until I saw you. Then I knew you were the girl I'd been waiting for. Where have you been all my life?

I know there's a difference in our ages. That doesn't matter to me. But I know it would matter to your parents. So perhaps we will never meet, and I will have to live with that sorrow. But I had to let you know my feelings, because my heart has told me you are my one and only, now and forever love.

There was no signature at the bottom. Cat's mind was racing as she visualized the boys she'd seen at Dream Burger. Was he one of the blond football players? The Tom Cruise look-alike? The long-haired one in the black jeans? And whoever he was, how had he learned her name?

She snapped her fingers. Marla's sister Chris. Maybe he was a friend of hers. Clutching the letter, she ran into Annie and Ben's bedroom where there was a phone extension. Her hand trembled as she punched in Marla's number.

Please, Marla, be home, she pleaded silently. She must have let it ring a hundred times. Finally, she gave up and went back to her room. She couldn't resist reading the letter again. This was the most romantic thing that had ever happened to her. She actually had a secret admirer! If she didn't tell someone about this, she'd explode.

At the sound of footsteps on the stairs, she ran to the door. Well, Becka was better than nobody. "Becka, come here. I've got something to show you."

Becka came in, and Cat handed her the letter. "Read this," she commanded.

She enjoyed watching Becka's expression as she read. Her eyes grew huge, and her mouth dropped open. "Cat! This is incredible! Who is he?"

"I don't know. There were so many guys at Dream Burger that day. High school boys, Becka! He could be sixteen, maybe seventeen years old!" She fell back on her bed. "And he's in love with me!"

"Wow," Becka breathed. "This is like something out of a book, or a movie. A secret love."

"I'm his 'one and only, now and forever love,'" Cat quoted from the letter. She'd already committed those words to memory.

"You have to find out who he is," Becka said excitedly. "You could go back to Dream Burger. Or hang around in front of the high school when classes get out."

Cat considered this. Then she shook her head. "No, that's childish. I don't want him to think I'm that anxious to find out who he is."

"Why not?" Becka asked.

Cat smiled at her kindly. Becka knew nothing about boys. "Never let a guy know you're available, Becka. Playing hard to get is always the best policy. Guys want what they think they can't get."

"Then what are you going to do?"

"I'll just have to be patient and wait until he comes after me." She shivered with delight. "If he's as much in love with me as he says he is, he won't give up."

"I wish I could be like you," Becka said. "I want to know how to make a boy like me."

"Anyone in particular?" Cat asked. Then she remembered. "Oh, yeah, Keith Doyle."

Becka struggled with her words. "Do you think . . . I know this sounds silly, but . . . could you teach me how to act with boys?" She looked up at Cat with that wistful, pathetic expression that usually got on Cat's nerves. But Cat was feeling so good, she found herself actually wanting to help.

"Sure. It's all a question of attitude, you know. If it doesn't come naturally to you, you can always fake it. Now, let me think . . ."

Josie came out of the girls' locker room, her knapsack slung over her shoulder. Todd and another player, Alex, were coming out of the boys' locker

42

room at the same time. "That was a good practice," Josie told them.

"Yeah," Todd said. "I could have sworn I saw Coach Matthews smile."

"Are you crazy?" Alex hooted. "You must be seeing things, buddy."

Josie grinned. Coach Matthews was famous for his grim expression. "You think it's going to be a good team?" she asked the boys.

"Yeah," Todd said. "But we sure could use someone with a good hook shot." He shook his head in regret. "Too bad we lost Keith Doyle."

The name rang a bell, but Josie couldn't think why. "How come he's not on the team anymore?"

"Grades," Alex told her. "He dropped to a C average last spring."

"There was that other business, too," Todd noted.

"What other business?" Josie asked.

Both boys looked uncomfortable. Alex grimaced. "There was a rumor going around that he copied from someone else's test paper and turned it in as his own."

"But nobody could prove it," Todd added. "The girl he copied from had a crush on him and wouldn't turn him in." He eyed Josie suspiciously. "How come you're so interested in Keith Doyle?"

"No reason," Josie said. "I'm just curious."

"Are you sure?" Alex asked. "He's got a reputation, you know."

"What kind of reputation?"

Now both boys were grinning, and they exchanged looks. "He's, you know, kind of a playboy," Todd told her. "He's always getting girls to fall for him."

"You don't want to get involved with him," Alex advised.

"I have no intention of getting involved with him," Josie said indignantly. "But thanks for the warning."

"Try it again," Cat ordered Becka.

Becka cocked her head at an angle, slightly dropped her eyelids, looked to the side, and formed a small smile.

Cat shook her head. "You still look like you've got a stiff neck."

Becka eyed her reflection in the mirror. Cat was right. "It doesn't look natural." She flopped down on the bed beside Cat. "I don't think acting like you is going to work."

"You don't have to act like me," Cat objected. "You can flirt in your own style."

"But I don't have a flirting style," Becka said. "I really want Keith to ask me to that dance. But I want him to ask me because he likes *me*. Not because I'm pretending to be you." She sighed. *"C'est difficile."*

"Huh?"

"I said 'it's difficult' in French. Did Mademoiselle Casalls tell you guys there's going to be another quiz next week?"

"Yeah." Cat pulled her feet up onto her bed and wrapped her arms around her knees. "I don't know how I'm going to study. I can't think about anything but my secret love."

"I don't blame you," Becka sighed.

"Listen," Cat said suddenly. "Don't tell anyone about my letter, okay?"

"Not even Josie?"

"Especially not Josie. She'll just tease me and make jokes about it."

"You're right," Becka agreed. "Josie wouldn't understand. I don't think she knows anything about romance."

"But she could," Cat mused. "You know, all she and Red need is a little push."

"Are you thinking about giving them the push?"

Cat grinned. "Why not? If Josie fell in love, she'd be a lot more feminine. And a lot easier to live with."

They heard Ben's call to dinner from downstairs.

"Now remember what I said," Cat cautioned as they ran down the stairs. "Not a word about you-know-what."

"Not a word," Becka promised. Having Cat's confidence gave her a warm glow. It wasn't too long ago that they couldn't bear to be in the same room. Becka and Cat joined Annie, Ben, and Josie at the table. Becka cast an appreciative eye on the main course.

"Mmm, chicken pie."

"Annie made it all by herself," Josie announced with the air of a proud parent.

"I think I got it right this time," Annie said as she began dishing it out.

"How was your day, girls?" Ben asked.

"We had a great basketball practice," Josie reported. "Oh, Cat, Todd said to tell you he'd call tonight."

"Okay," Cat said.

"Cat, don't you like your chicken pie?" Annie asked anxiously.

"What? Oh, sure, it's great. I guess I'm just not very hungry."

"Uh-oh," Ben said. "Isn't loss of appetite a sign of being in love?"

"Not for me," Annie said cheerfully. "Every time I fell in love, I ate like a pig. When I first met Ben I gained five pounds."

"Maybe Becka's in love, then," Josie remarked.

Becka looked at her plate and flushed when she realized she'd already devoured her dinner. Annie and Ben were looking at her with interest.

"Well, there is a boy I kind of like," she confessed.

"Who is he?" Ben asked.

"Now, Ben, don't pry," Annie chided him. "When Becka wants to tell us about him, she will."

"It'll be interesting to see how Josie reacts to being in love," Ben said in a teasing voice.

"I'll be sick to my stomach," Josie replied promptly.

"Josie!" Cat exclaimed. "Not at the table, *please*!"

46

"Don't worry. It's not going to happen any time soon. If ever."

Cat turned her head and gave Becka a significant wink.

"What's going on at school?" Annie asked.

"There's going to be a dance," Cat said.

Annie clapped her hands. "Your first dance! Oh, we have to go shopping."

"For what?" Ben asked.

"Ben! We've got three daughters going to their first dance! Three daughters means three new outfits."

"Not three," Josie said. "I'm not going."

"How do you know?" Cat said. "Maybe Red will ask you."

Josie made a face. "I'm sure Red isn't any more interested in going to a dance than I am."

"Are you going, Becka?" Annie asked.

"If somebody asks me."

"You mean, you have to have a date?" Ben asked.

"You don't have to," Cat told him. "But everybody does."

Annie shook her head. "Kids grow up so fast nowadays."

"Too fast, in my opinion," Ben said. He turned to Annie. "Did you hear about that place on Green Street? The one that's letting in underage kids? What's it called?"

"Escapade," Cat answered.

Ben frowned. "How do you know about it?"

"I haven't been there," Cat said hastily. "I just heard some older kids talking about it."

"Something should be done about that place," Annie commented.

"Nobody's caught them letting the kids in," Ben said. "And I doubt that any kids will be going to the police to confess."

After dinner, the girls cleared the table. Once they were alone in the kitchen, Josie turned to Becka. "Who's this boy you kind of like?"

Cat answered for her. "Keith Doyle."

"Keith Doyle! Gross!"

"What's gross about him?" Becka asked indignantly.

"I heard some of the guys talking about him. They said he plays around, he flirts with everyone. He gets girls to fall madly in love with him."

"Oh, *please*," Cat snorted. "All boys do that." Her eyes grew misty. "Until they get older. Then, one day, they find their one and only, now and forever love."

Josie brushed that aside. "I heard worse about Keith Doyle. There's a rumor that he cheats."

"I don't believe that," Becka said stoutly. "If he cheated, he wouldn't be making D's in French."

"What's the big deal, anyway?" Cat challenged Josie. "Okay, maybe he cheats a little. So what? He's cute, and he's popular, and Becka likes him. So mind your own business!"

"I'm just warning her," Josie countered. "You've

got to watch out for guys like that. If you ask me, he sounds kind of sleazy."

"Nobody asked you," Cat shot back.

"Come on, you guys, stop it," Becka pleaded. "Look, he hasn't even asked me out."

"Yet," Cat added.

Josie threw up her hands and went back out to the dining room. Becka stared after her thoughtfully. "You know, Cat, I think you're right about Josie."

"Right about what?"

"She *does* need to fall in love."

Four

Becka was in a rush to get to French class. She'd noticed that Keith's locker was right by the door and that he usually stopped there just before class. Surely she wouldn't look peculiar hanging out in front of her own classroom. She'd be in a perfect position to strike up a conversation.

But about what? She was mentally exploring various topics as she ran down the stairs. Then she heard her name being called.

She turned to see a small, thin girl with uneven bangs and glasses slipping down her nose hurrying down the stairs to catch up with her. "Hi, Louise."

Louise was in Becka's homeroom and had been one of the first friends Becka had made at her new school. Louise waved the latest issue of the *Green Ga-*

zette, which had just come out that day. "Becka, I just wanted to tell you how much I liked this editorial."

Becka edged down another step. "Thanks," she said hurriedly, "but I didn't have anything to do with it. Jason was the one who wrote it."

"I think the idea of an honor code is excellent," Louise went on. She started talking about how it would cut down on cheating and make students think twice if they were tempted. Becka kept glancing down the stairs, but Louise didn't take the hint, and Becka didn't want to be rude.

When Becka finally got away, she dashed down the remainder of the stairs. But she was too late. Just as she tore around the corner, she saw Keith slamming his locker door and going into the room.

Becka slid into her seat just as the bell rang. There was only time for a brief hi to Patty before Mademoiselle Casalls started talking. Becka gazed at the back of Keith's head, but she couldn't afford to daydream about him. They were doing irregular verb conjugations that day, which required a lot of concentration.

"For tomorrow, Friday, you will answer the questions on page sixty," the teacher announced at the end of class. "And do not forget about the test on Monday."

The bell rang. Becka watched wistfully as Keith ran out of the room. Patty turned around and read her expression. "You've got it bad."

Becka didn't even attempt to deny it. She gathered

her books and left the room with Patty. "Cat tried to give me flirting lessons," she confessed.

Patty laughed. "I'll bet she's a good teacher. She's an authority on that subject."

"But I was a crummy student. It just didn't feel right to me. If I tried to fake it, I'd look goofy. Patty, how can I get him to notice me?"

Patty twisted a strand of her short, fair hair, which meant she was thinking. Then she clutched Becka's arm and pulled her out of the flow of moving students. "I've got it! You're a whiz in French, right?"

"I do okay," Becka said modestly.

"Keith stinks in French, right?"

Becka drew back. "Well, I wouldn't put it like *that*."

"Oh, come on, I've seen the way Mademoiselle Casalls looks at him when she hands back the quizzes. Why don't you offer to help him?"

Becka stared at her. "You mean, be a tutor?" She gasped. "That's brilliant! I don't know why I didn't think of that. You know, that's how my parents met. Annie tutored Ben in algebra when they were in school."

"And look how they turned out," Patty said. She gave Becka a light punch on the shoulder. "Go for it!"

For the rest of the day, Becka gave only half her attention to her classes. The rest she devoted to imagining her approach to Keith. She would accidentally-on-purpose run into him at his locker after the last bell. She'd casually make a comment about the up-coming quiz. With any luck, he'd say something about dreading it. Then, acting like the idea had just occurred to her, she'd hit him with her offer.

Throughout her last class, she kept her eye on the clock. She was poised to move as soon as class was over. When the bell rang, she shot out of the room like a marathon runner who'd just heard the gun.

She turned the last corner, expecting to see Keith at the end of the hall. But he wasn't there. Becka strolled down the hall very slowly, her eyes glued to his locker. The corridor was so crowded with kids pulling books and coats out of their lockers, she was able to go back and forth, up and down the hall, without attracting attention. But after a few minutes, the hall began to clear as students left. Soon only a handful were still hanging around. And at least one of them was beginning to eye her curiously.

Becka was passing the room where her French class was held when she happened to glance through the door's window. Her heart leaped. There was Keith, at Mademoiselle Casalls' desk. The teacher wasn't there. He was probably waiting to have a meeting with her.

Becka thought quickly. She could say she left a book in her desk. Before she could lose her nerve, she put her hand on the knob and walked in.

Keith jumped back from the desk with a stricken expression. But when he saw who had come in, relief crossed his face and he grinned.

A rush of excitement filled Becka. *He's glad to see me,* she thought.

"Whew," he said. "For a second, I thought you were Mademoiselle Casalls."

"Isn't that who you're waiting for?" Becka asked.

He laughed as if she'd just said something funny. It was then that Becka realized the teacher's desk drawer was open. "What are you doing?"

He hesitated for a moment, then winked at Becka. "I was just looking for a copy of Monday's French quiz," he replied.

Now it was Becka's turn to laugh. "Very funny." But then, as Keith continued to rifle through the papers in the desk, a cold chill shot through her. It dawned on her that maybe he wasn't joking.

"Keith! You—you're not serious, are you?"

He glanced up and gave her a disarming smile. "You may be a genius, but some of us need a little advantage when it comes to quizzes."

Becka was dumbstruck. But even in her shock, she knew how Cat would react in a situation like this. She'd laugh it off. She might even offer to help search the drawer! But there was no way Becka couldn't let her feelings show. "Keith, that's cheating!" she blurted out.

"Oh, I'm not going to steal it," he assured her. "I just want to peek at some of the questions."

"It's still wrong," Becka insisted.

His smile faded slightly. "Wait a minute. Are you

54

going to tell on me? I didn't think you were a goody-goody."

"I'm not," Becka protested. "And I didn't say I was going to tell anyone." She saw a copy of the school newspaper lying on the desk. "If we had an honor code, I'd *have* to turn you in."

"But we don't have an honor code, right?"

Becka nodded slowly. "Right. Not yet, at least. But that doesn't mean it's okay to cheat."

She jumped as Keith slammed the drawer shut. "It's not in there anyway," he muttered.

Becka gazed at him sorrowfully. Then she turned away and started toward the door. "Wait a minute," Keith said. Becka paused and looked back.

Keith was smiling again. "I guess you think I'm some kind of criminal, huh?"

Becka didn't know what to say. She stared down at the floor. Keith came closer, touched her chin, and lifted her face so she had to look right up into his eyes.

"Listen, I got tossed off the basketball team because of my grades. But Coach Matthews says he'll let me back on before the season starts if my grades improve this month. Becka, playing basketball means a lot to me."

Becka swallowed. He sounded so sincere, so anxious. And his eyes . . . She could have sworn they were misting over.

"So you see, I've got to do well on this test."

Becka's insides were turning to mush. He was

pleading for her to understand. Who was she to pass judgment on him? He'd been driven to this act out of desperation, like someone who robs a bank to feed his hungry children.

Still, she couldn't let him think she approved of this sort of behavior. "There . . . there are other ways to get your grades up."

Keith hung his head. "You wouldn't believe how hard I study. But this French stuff just doesn't sink in. I guess I'm not the smartest guy in the world."

Becka caught her breath. Here it was, the perfect opportunity. "Maybe I could help you."

He looked at her with hope in his eyes. "Yeah?"

Becka nodded. "I could tutor you. We could get together, um, this weekend . . ." Her voice trailed off. Was she imagining it, or had the hope faded?

But then he smiled. "Yeah, okay. What about tomorrow night?"

"Tomorrow night?" Becka repeated.

"What's the matter? You got a date?"

"A date?" Becka wanted to kick herself. She was making it sound like the possibility of having a date was nonexistent. "No, I don't have a date *Friday* night," she said, emphasizing the Friday. "You could come over to my house."

"Great," he said. "You can try to pound some knowledge into my head, and then we'll go to Luigi's. How about if I come by around five?"

"Okay."

"It's a date," he said.

A date. The words were ringing in her ears long after he walked out of the room. She had a date with Keith Doyle. Okay, maybe it wasn't a *real* date. But it was close. Closer than she'd ever been to a date before.

Sitting across from Marla in Brownies, Cat waited to see her friend's reaction to her story. She wasn't disappointed.

Marla put a hand to her heart and moaned in rapture. "Cat! That's so amazing! Honestly, I've never heard of anything so incredibly romantic before!"

"Will you find out from Chris if anyone asked her my name?"

"Absolutely. But I think she would have told me if anyone had."

"How else could he have found out my name?"

Marla thought about it. "Let's see . . . he couldn't have looked you up in the yearbook, because you weren't in last year's. Maybe he knows someone in junior high." Her eyes widened. "Maybe he hired a private investigator."

The idea had never occurred to Cat. "Do you think any guy would go to that much trouble to find out a girl's name?"

"Why not? A man would go to the ends of the earth to find the woman he loves."

Cat stirred her ice cream soda. "I wonder if I'll ever meet him. Even if I did, Annie and Ben would never let me go out with a high school boy."

"How tragic," Marla said. "Destined never to meet, never to share your love. Star-crossed lovers."

Cat experienced a feeling of melancholy that wasn't exactly unpleasant. She felt like a heroine in a sad but beautiful love story. "Star-crossed lovers," she echoed. "Like Romeo and Juliet."

"At least you still have Todd," Marla said.

That brought Cat back to earth. "Todd . . . can you imagine him calling me his one and only, now and forever love? All he ever calls me is 'babe.' " She shuddered.

"Come on, he's not so bad," Marla argued. "He's one of the cutest boys at school, he's a jock, and he's got a nice personality."

"Yeah, I know. I just wish I could get him to be more romantic."

"I'm sure you can if you try," Marla said.

"Hi, Marla, Cat."

The girls looked up. Heather stood there, with Blair Chase and Eve Dedham.

"Hi," Cat and Marla replied.

"What's new?" Heather asked pleasantly. Behind her, Blair muffled a giggle. Eve just looked uncomfortable.

"Not much," Cat replied, her eyes darting among the girls.

"Well, see you around."

As soon as they were out of earshot, Cat leaned across the table. "What was *that* all about? Why is she so friendly all of sudden?"

"I don't know," Marla said. "But there's something I don't like about it. I still can't believe she's given up on getting Todd back."

"You think she's got some sort of rotten scheme cooking?" Cat asked.

Marla shrugged. "Maybe it's just my suspicious mind. But I think you should keep an eye on Todd."

Cat got up. "You know, Todd's working at his father's store right now. Maybe I'll go by there and see if he wants to take a break."

Marla nodded in approval. "Good idea. Don't let this secret admirer distract you. After all, *he* can't take you to the dance."

The girls separated, and Cat walked down the street to Sports Stuff. The store was quiet. Todd was standing by the counter, looking bored. He brightened when Cat came in.

"Hi, babe," he greeted her.

Cat winced, but she forced a bright smile. "Can you get away for a little while?"

"I'll ask my Dad." He left the counter and went to the back of the store. Cat idly picked up a card lying on the counter.

In fancy, curly script, it read: You are cordially invited to enjoy a complimentary dinner for two at La Petite Maison.

La Petite Maison. Cat had absorbed enough French to know this meant "the little house." But she also knew what La Petite Maison was, and it definitely wasn't any little house. It was the only really elegant, fancy French restaurant in Green Falls. Annie had told Cat that Ben had taken her there for their anniversary last year.

"Hello, Cat," Mr. Murphy boomed. The heavyset, balding man beamed at her jovially. Cat wondered if this was what Todd would look like someday.

"Hi, Mr. Murphy," she said. "I was just wondering if Todd could take a break."

"Sure," he said. "And you kids could do me a favor while you're out." He took out his wallet and turned to Todd. "I need you to pick up a birthday gift for me to give your mother. She likes a perfume called Everlasting. I think you can get it at Harrison's."

"Okay," Todd said, pocketing the money.

Cat pointed to the card on the counter. "Are you taking her to La Petite Maison for her birthday?"

He shook his head in regret. "No, Mrs. Murphy and I are both on diets." He picked up the card. "Todd, why don't you and Cat use this? It would be a shame to waste it." The tinkle of a bell indicated the arrival of a customer, and Mr. Murphy left to wait on him.

Cat clapped her hands in glee. "Oh, Todd, I'd love to go to La Petite Maison."

Todd looked at the card. "Is this one of those places where a guy has to wear a coat and tie?"

"Uh, yes . . . but you'd look great in a coat and tie! And it will be so nice to get really dressed up for a change."

60

Todd frowned. "French food? That's stuff like snails and frogs' legs."

"I'm sure they have other things, too," Cat said.

Todd still didn't look very happy about the idea. "This isn't my kind of place."

"How do you know? You've never been there!"

Todd sighed. "Well, if you really want to go . . ."

"I do! How about tomorrow night? There's no football game."

He shoved the card in his pocket. "Yeah, okay."

Cat rewarded him with her very best killer smile. They left the store and walked around the corner to Harrison's Department Store. Just inside, there were mannequins displaying men's suits from Italy. Even without faces, the mannequins looked suave and debonair. "Todd, how do you like this?" she asked.

Todd glanced at the suit and snorted. "Looks like something a sissy would wear."

She should have known. "Come on, Todd, let's go find the perfume."

He hesitated as they neared the perfume counter. "Hey, Cat, could you ask for the stuff?" He fumbled in his pocket for the money. "I feel stupid buying perfume."

Cat rolled her eyes. "Todd, guys buy perfume for women all the time."

"*I* don't. Look, just do it for me, okay?"

Taking the money, Cat went to the counter. "I'd like a bottle of Everlasting, please." While the saleswoman went to get it, Cat examined the sample bot-

61

tles of perfume. She selected one and sprayed a little on her wrist. Then she breathed the scent in deeply.

It was glorious, flowery and feminine. She could see herself walking into a place like La Petite Maison, trailing clouds of this heavenly scent behind her. Men would look up, attracted by the fragrance. Maybe she could save her allowance and buy some. Or maybe she could get it as a gift. This scent could become her signature. Every time people smelled it, they'd know Cat Morgan was around.

"Here you are, dear," the saleswoman said. Cat paid for the perfume and joined Todd, who was leaning against a pillar.

He sniffed. "You smell funny."

Cat closed her eyes and counted to ten. Turning Todd into a romantic was going to be even harder than she thought.

Five

It was a few minutes after five on Friday when Josie burst into Morgan's Country Foods. "Sorry I'm late," she said breathlessly.

"That's okay," Annie said. "It's been quiet. Do you want to unpack that box of preserves on the counter?"

Cat wrinkled her nose as Josie came closer. "Ick, you smell like a horse."

"That's not surprising," Josie replied. "Considering the fact that I've been on one for the past hour."

Annie laughed. "Just don't get too close to any customers, if we have any. How was your ride?"

"Great. With all the basketball practices, I haven't been on a horse in . . . well, it feels like ages."

"That's not true," Cat said. "You ride Maybelline all the time."

"That doesn't count," Josie replied.

"Poor old Maybelline," Annie sighed. "Ben and I didn't know anything about horses when we bought her. We couldn't understand why the farmer was selling her so cheap. Now we know."

"Sometimes I wonder if she's really a horse," Josie said. "Maybe she's a cow in disguise. Anyway, that's how she moves."

Cat eyed Josie in distaste. "How did you get that sweaty riding her?"

"I wasn't riding Maybelline," Josie said. "Red let me take Dusty, and I got him up to a real gallop."

"A gallop?" Worry lines appeared on Annie's forehead. "Josie, you haven't been riding that long. I don't like the idea of your racing around on a horse by yourself."

"I wasn't by myself," Josie assured her. "Red was with me. He took their new horse, Belinda."

"Well, that's better," Annie said, turning back to the pickle jars she was labeling.

"Much better," Cat echoed. She gave Josie a sly smile, which Josie responded to by sticking out her tongue.

"Cat, what time is Todd coming for you?" Annie asked.

"Six-thirty. Can I go now? I want to take a long bubble bath and French braid my hair."

Josie raised her eyebrows. "For Todd? The last time you went out with him you spent five minutes getting ready."

"This is different," Cat said. "Tonight is going to be special, not the usual Friday night."

"I think you'll enjoy La Petite Maison," Annie commented. "It's very elegant."

Josie chuckled. "Todd Murphy at La Petite Maison."

"What's so funny about that?" Cat demanded.

"I just can't picture Todd eating in a place whose name he can't pronounce."

Cat glared at her in annoyance. "I'm going to get ready." She flounced out of the store, practically colliding with Ben, who was on his way in. "Sorry," she called as she passed him.

"Why is she in such a rush?" he asked Annie.

"Big date tonight with Todd," she replied.

He shook his head sadly. "Seems like we just got our daughters, and already the boys are standing in line to take them away from us."

Annie smiled. "Did you meet Becka's friend?"

"Yeah, he just arrived. He seems like a nice enough boy."

Josie's head jerked up. "What's his name?"

"Keith something," Ben replied. "Becka's tutoring him in French." He winked at his wife. "And we all know what that can lead to."

"Do you know him, Josie?" Annie asked.

"Not really. I know *about* him." Josie tried to keep her voice even, but something in her expression must have betrayed her thoughts.

"Is there something about him we should know?" Annie asked.

Josie bit her lip. She could tell Annie and Ben what she'd heard about Keith Doyle, and they could discourage Becka's interest. But Becka would *kill* her. No, she'd better handle this herself.

"Oh, it's nothing. I'm just thinking about all this homework I've got. There should be a law against assigning homework on weekends."

"Why don't you go get started on it now?" Ben suggested. "Then you'll get it over with and have the weekend free."

That was exactly what Josie wanted to hear. "Thanks," she said and ran out. When she walked into the house, she could hear the murmur of voices coming from the dining room. She paused, uncertain about what to do.

Why was she so worried anyway? If it had been Cat in there with a boy, she wouldn't be the least bit concerned. But Becka—she was so gullible. It would be just like her to be swept off her feet by some phony Romeo.

But Josie couldn't exactly burst in and order Keith out of the house. She had to play it cool. She'd scope out the situation and then decide what needed to be done.

Shoving her hands in her pockets and whistling, she ambled into the dining room. Everything looked pretty innocent so far. Keith was slumped in a chair, his elbows on the table and his eyes glazed over.

Becka, sitting next to him, was reading out loud from the French textbook propped in front of her. Both of them looked up as Josie entered.

"Hi," Becka said. "Josie, do you know Keith?"

Josie was about to say "only by reputation," but she held it back. "Hi, Keith."

He smiled. "So you're the famous Josie Morgan."

"Famous?" Josie asked, momentarily put off by his tone and his killer smile. The guy was dripping with charm.

"Well, you're the first girl ever on the basketball team. You must be some athlete."

Flattery will get you nowhere with me, Josie thought. But being perfectly objective, she could see how he'd earned his reputation. "What are you guys doing?"

"Studying French," Becka said. "We've got a quiz on Monday."

"Becka's trying to drum some irregular verbs through my thick skull," Keith added.

"Oh, Keith," Becka remonstrated. "Don't put yourself down like that."

Josie didn't like the way Becka was looking at him, like a lovesick calf. She pulled out a chair and plunked herself down. "Maybe I can help."

"But you're taking Spanish," Becka protested.

"Spanish, French, what's the difference? They're both foreign."

Keith tossed back his head and laughed. Josie fixed steely eyes on him. "It wasn't *that* funny," she muttered.

Becka consulted her book. "Okay, let's conjugate the verb *aller*." To Josie, she said, "That means 'to go.'"

Keith pretended to pout. "Do we have to?"

Becka nodded. "Come on, Keith. I know this will be on the quiz."

"Haven't we already worked enough for today?" Keith asked plaintively.

Becka frowned. "You've only been here fifteen minutes!"

"Okay," Keith said with a sigh. "We'll work for an hour. And then we'll go to Luigi's, okay?"

Becka nodded happily. Josie drummed her fingers on the table. So this wasn't just a tutoring session. They were going to Luigi's, where Green Falls Junior High boys took girls for dates on Friday nights.

Becka sniffed. "I smell something funny."

"It's me," Josie said. "I've been riding." She stood up. "I'm going to take a shower."

"I think Cat's in the bathroom," Becka told her.

"I'll chase her out. Excuse me."

She took the stairs two at a time. Sounds of splashing and singing came from behind the bathroom door, but Josie ignored them. She went directly into Ben and Annie's room, picked up the phone, and dialed.

"Hi, Red, it's Josie."

"Hi, what's up?"

"You want to go to Luigi's?"

There was a silence on the other end. "Luigi's? Now?"

Josie knew why he sounded puzzled, and she couldn't blame him. She and Red had been to Luigi's a zillion times, but not on a Friday night. Not on a date night. "Look, I can't explain now, but it's important."

"Well, okay."

"Come on over in an hour." She hung up the phone and smiled grimly. At least she'd be there to keep an eye on that slimy charmer.

"What are you smiling about?" Cat stood in the doorway, her hair wrapped in a towel.

"Just thinking about something."

"Did you see Becka downstairs with Keith?"

"Yeah."

The corners of Cat's lips turned up. "Better get your act together, Josie, or you'll be the only unattached Morgan girl."

"You mean, I'll be the only *sane* Morgan girl," Josie retorted. They both turned as Becka came running up the stairs.

"Did Keith leave already?" Cat asked in dismay.

"No," Becka said. "I just have to get my French dictionary."

"Well, don't leave him alone too long," Cat scolded. "How's it going down there?"

"Okay, I guess. I don't know if I'm helping him all that much. I think he's got a mental block when it comes to French."

"I'm not asking about *that*," Cat said impatiently. "I mean, how's it going with you and Keith?"

Becka smiled shyly. "He's taking me to Luigi's."

"Excellent!" Cat exclaimed.

"Is it okay if Red and I go with you?" Josie asked.

"Sure," Becka said. "That'll be fun." She was getting that dreamy look in her eyes that Josie found so irritating. "Just think, Josie, all those years when we were roommates at the orphanage . . . who would have thought one day we'd be double-dating?" She sailed off into her room.

Josie scowled. When she turned to Cat, her frown deepened. "What are you smirking at me like that for?"

"You and Red," Cat replied promptly. "Going to Luigi's on a Friday night, huh?" As she turned to go into her room, she sang out, "I told you so!"

For once, Cat's fantasies had become a reality. La Petite Maison was everything she'd imagined it to be and more. It was a small restaurant, with dim lighting and candles that cast a pale glow on each lace-covered table. Soft violin music blended with the low murmur of conversation and the tinkling of glasses. A man in a black suit with a bow tie had seated them, and he'd pulled Cat's chair out for her. Cat hoped Todd had noticed this, but she doubted it.

There was a gold-framed mirror on the wall by her table, and Cat caught her reflection. In all modesty, she had to say she'd never looked better. The dark green dress made her eyes shine like emeralds, and the French braid made her look at least sixteen, she thought.

Across from her, Todd was tugging at his collar and shifting around in his chair.

"What's the matter?" she asked.

"I hate ties," he muttered. "And these chairs are too hard." He opened the menu. "It's so dark in here I can't even read this." He grabbed the candle and pulled it closer. "Hey, this is in French!"

"It's a French restaurant," Cat said.

"Yeah, well, I'm American. Jeez, look at these prices."

Was he going to complain all evening? "Todd, you don't have to pay, remember?" She opened her own menu. Once, Mademoiselle Casalls had brought a menu from a French restaurant to class, and she'd explained what all the different words meant. Too bad Cat hadn't paid much attention.

She was distracted by a young couple who were being seated at the table next to them. They couldn't be that much older than she and Todd were, she thought. Maybe five years. But five years certainly made a big difference. The guy was gazing intently at his date, as if he were hypnotized. Cat strained to hear what he was saying.

"You're looking very beautiful tonight," he said.

"Thank you, darling," she replied.

Cat sighed. "Todd . . ."

He was still staring at the menu. "Yeah?"

"Do you like my hair this way?"

"Yeah, sure." His eyes hadn't even left the menu.

"Should I wear it like this for the dance at school?"

"Sure, if you want to."

He was *impossible*. A waiter appeared by their table. "May I take your order?"

Cat looked at the menu again. She could say she wasn't ready, but then, she could study this menu for an hour and still not be ready.

"May I explain some of our dishes to you?" the waiter asked kindly.

"Oh, no, that won't be necessary," Cat replied. "I'll have, um, the *escargots* and the *canard*."

She didn't know if she'd pronounced the words properly, and the waiter gave no indication whether or not she had. "And for you, sir?"

"Uh, I guess I'll have the same thing."

As soon as the waiter left them, Todd asked, "What are we getting?"

Cat didn't want to tell him she didn't have the slightest idea. "Let it be a surprise."

Todd tugged at his collar again. "Why can't they have decent music in here?"

Cat glanced at the couple next to them again. Now their hands were touching across the table. Cat let her own hand sneak across the table. Todd didn't notice. He was counting the silver by his plate. "What do we need so many forks for?"

"Todd . . ."

"Huh?"

"How's the basketball team coming along?"

Answering that question kept him occupied until the waiter returned. Ceremoniously, he placed silver dishes in front of them.

Cat stared at the little shells. In each was nestled a glob of something that looked pretty disgusting. She hoped her face didn't reveal her reaction.

Todd didn't even try to hide his feelings. "What's that?"

"*Escargots*, sir," the waiter replied. Then he translated. "Snails."

Todd's face turned a rather interesting shade of green.

Luigi's was packed and noisy. Kids were hopping from one table to another. Becka sat in the corner of a booth and picked a cold piece of pepperoni off the remnants of a pizza. Across from her, Josie and Red were engaged in a lively argument over some football game they'd seen on TV. Keith had wandered off to talk to a guy at another table.

"There're Cat and Todd," Josie said suddenly.

Becka turned. Todd was in the process of pulling off his tie as he strode toward them. He had a broad, relaxed grin on his face, as if he'd been lost in the woods and finally discovered his campsite. Cat walked behind him, an expression of resignation on her face.

"Hi guys," Todd said when he reached their booth. "Can we squeeze in?"

Red and Josie moved over to make room for him, and Cat slipped in next to Becka. "Where's Keith?" she asked.

"Around," Becka replied. "What are you doing here? I thought you were going to that French restaurant."

"We went," Cat said. "But Todd's still hungry."

Todd snorted and turned to Red. "You wouldn't believe what they call a meal in that joint. It's not enough to feed a baby. Can I have a slice of that pizza?"

"It's cold," Josie warned him.

Todd didn't care. He took a slice and practically crammed the whole thing in his mouth.

"Hiya, buddy!" Keith had reappeared. Todd was obviously surprised to see him.

"How'd you get out of the house? I thought you were grounded for life after your last report card!"

Cat hopped out of the booth and let Keith get in next to Becka. Becka shot her a grateful look. Cat was becoming remarkably sensitive.

Keith tossed an arm loosely around Becka's shoulder. If there was such a thing as heaven on earth, Becka had just found it.

"Becka here rescued me," Keith told Todd. "When I told my father I was being tutored, he let me out." He gave Becka an endearing smile. "Thanks, Becka."

"You're welcome," Becka said. "I'm happy to tutor you anytime you want."

"You mean it?" Keith gave her a little squeeze. "This is great. Whenever I want to get out of the house, Becka will provide me with an excuse."

Becka laughed uncertainly.

"You going to be playing basketball this season?" Red asked.

"If I can get the grades up," Keith said.

Todd shook a finger at Becka and pretended to be stern. "You better do a good job. The whole team's counting on you."

"I'm willing if Keith is," Becka said. She liked the way Keith gazed at her appreciatively.

"I'm going to hold you to that," he said. "Hey, there's Alex." Todd and Red joined Keith and headed across the room.

Becka didn't miss the way Josie's eyes followed Keith and the way they narrowed. "Why don't you like him?"

"I just don't think he's all that serious about learning French," Josie replied. "It seems to me he wasn't paying much attention when you were working at home."

"That's okay," Cat said. "It just means his mind was on Becka."

"You really think so?" Becka asked eagerly.

"Absolutely."

"How was dinner at La Petite Maison?" Josie asked. "I guess Todd wasn't too crazy about it."

Cat's smile disappeared. "I don't think Todd's mature enough to appreciate a place like that. Not like—" She stopped suddenly.

"Not like who?" Josie asked.

"No one."

But Becka caught the glint in Cat's eye and knew she was thinking about her mysterious admirer. She gave Cat a knowing, sympathetic look.

Red returned and started to sit down. "Wait," Josie said. "Let me get out first. I have to go to the bathroom." She climbed out of the booth. "Too many sodas."

A look of agony crossed Cat's face and she closed her eyes. "I can't believe she said that in front of a boy," she whispered to Becka.

Becka nodded fervently. She herself might not have had much experience with boys, but even she knew you *never* told a boy what you were going to the bathroom for.

Red sat down, and Cat smiled brightly at him. "I'm glad to see you and Josie out together."

Red looked at her blankly. "We're together a lot. You know that."

Cat uttered a tinkling laugh. "Oh, come on, you know what I mean. Out on a *date*."

Red just stared at her.

"And it's about time," Cat went on. "She's been waiting ages for this."

Becka watched Red's freckles begin to merge. "She . . . she has?" he stammered.

76

"Shh," Becka hissed. Josie was returning. Red got out of the booth. "Uh, I'll be right back."

Josie looked after him curiously. "Why is his face so pink?"

"Maybe because he was thinking about you," Cat said. "Really, Josie, you should be more aware of his feelings."

"You're nuts," Josie said succinctly.

Before long, it was time to go. They all left together and started up Main Street. Cat lagged behind the crowd.

"Cat, come on," Josie called.

Becka turned and saw Cat staring across the street. She followed the direction of her eyes and realized they were focused on Dream Burger. There was an oddly wistful smile on her face. Becka was the only one who knew what she was thinking.

Six

As Becka took her seat in French on Monday, Patty turned around. "I bet I know how you're feeling right now."

"I studied pretty hard," Becka said.

Patty grinned. "I'm not talking about the test. I heard you went out with Keith Friday night."

It was amazing how fast stories spread. "It was no big deal," Becka said in an offhand way. "I was tutoring him. Then we went to Luigi's."

"That's still a date," Patty insisted. "Do you think he's going to ask you to the dance?"

Becka dropped her mask of nonchalance. "I don't know. Keep your fingers crossed for me."

Patty's voice dropped to a whisper. "Here he comes now."

Unlike most of the kids, who raced to their desks

and opened their books for last-minute cramming, Keith strolled in with an air of confidence. Becka's stomach started jumping when she realized he wasn't going to his usual seat. He was heading directly toward her. He dropped his books on the desk just behind hers. "Anyone sitting here?"

Dumbly, Becka shook her head.

"Well, someone's sitting here now," he announced, hitting her with the full force of his smile.

Patty, who was listening, put a hand over her mouth and looked at Becka wide-eyed. Becka understood her reaction. Whenever a boy liked a girl, he moved to the seat just in back of hers so he could whisper in her ear and pass notes. It was a tradition of long standing at Green Falls Junior High. In fact, Cat had a boy sitting behind her in every one of her classes.

Now Keith was sitting behind Becka. He was announcing to everyone that he was interested in her.

Becka turned slightly and offered a smile. The smile he flashed back was different from his usual one. It suggested that they shared a special secret. Becka couldn't think of one thing to say. Luckily, she didn't have time to say anything. Mademoiselle Casalls walked in.

"Please put away the books, boys and girls," she said pleasantly. "I am certain you are all well prepared for this test, and you will all do splendidly."

A voice whispered in Becka's ear. "What an optimist."

Becka bit her lip so she wouldn't giggle.

"I will now distribute the tests, but please do not begin them until I say it is time. You will have the entire period to complete them."

"Do we get extra points if we finish early?" Keith murmured.

This time Becka had to clamp her hand over her mouth. How was she ever going to concentrate on this test with Keith whispering in her ear? Even if he didn't, just knowing he was there was going to make her nervous.

She wanted to turn and wish him good luck, but she couldn't. The teacher was getting closer. She placed a test facedown on Becka's desk, but she was looking past her.

"I see you have changed your seat, Keith," she said.

"Yes. I mean *oui*. Is that okay?"

Becka didn't understand why Mademoiselle Casalls hesitated. People changed seats all the time. Finally she nodded, handed him a test, and moved on.

"All right, you may commence," she announced.

The room became silent except for the scratching of pens and pencils. With all the mental power she could gather, Becka forced Keith out of her mind.

The questions were about what she'd expected. She was particularly glad to see that they had to conjugate the verb *aller*. Surely Keith would remember that.

She finished before the end of the period and

spent the rest of the time going over her answers. Then the bell rang. Students dropped the tests on the teacher's desk as they went out.

Keith left the room before Becka, but he was waiting just outside the door. Behind his back, Patty gave Becka a thumbs-up sign and scurried away.

"How'd you do?" Keith asked.

"Okay, I think," Becka said. "How about you?"

"Okay," Keith said, his eyes twinkling. "I think."

"Did the tutoring . . . was I a help?" Becka asked shyly.

"You bet," Keith replied.

"Then maybe we can study together again sometime."

"Yeah, maybe." Keith gave her a salute. "See ya."

As he walked away, Becka realized they'd been standing just under a poster announcing the upcoming dance. She wondered if he'd noticed it.

Cat sat on the gym bleachers with the other members of the pep club and half listened to committee reports. She was thinking about her success as a matchmaker. She had been pleased when Becka reported that Keith had changed his seat in their French class. It was a good sign. She was going to have to work more on Josie and Red. Josie wasn't exactly being cooperative. But with Cat's help, Josie and Becka could both become . . . well, maybe not as popular as Cat, but socially acceptable, at least.

She remembered so clearly how both of them had

embarrassed her when they first started at Green Falls Junior High. They were definitely improving. Getting them both a decent love life would make the biggest difference.

As for her own love life . . . well, she had Todd. But she couldn't get that secret admirer out of her mind. Would she ever hear from him again?

She felt Marla's elbow in her ribs. "Get a load of Heather."

The pep club president was prancing down the bleachers. She had on a fabulous outfit, a long pink sweater with a short purple skirt and purple leather boots. She had a new haircut, too. And she was looking very pleased with herself.

"What's she so happy about?" Cat wondered out loud.

Heather stood before the crowd and gave them all a warm, toothy smile. "I just want to remind you all that the pep club is cosponsoring the dance next week along with the student council. So we have to support the dance, and I want to see every one of you there."

"Too bad she can't provide dates for us to go with," Britt muttered.

"Who is *she* going with?" Cat asked.

"I don't know," Marla said. "But I'll find out."

The meeting was over, and Cat left with her friends. Passing the library, she saw Red coming out. "You guys go on ahead," she told the others. "I'll catch up."

She waved to Red. "Hi. Going home?"

"No, I'm meeting Josie at the gym."

Cat clapped her hands. "Oh, Red, I'm so glad!"

Her enthusiasm startled him. "Why?"

"Red, weren't you listening to me at Luigi's? Josie likes you."

"Of course she likes me," Red said patiently. "We're friends."

Cat sighed. "You know, Red, for a smart guy you can be really dense. Josie *likes* you. Get it? Okay, maybe she doesn't act like it, but I'm her sister. I *know*."

Red suddenly became very interested in his shoes. "Uh, yeah, okay. Look, I better get going."

Well, she'd definitely gotten through that time, Cat decided as she ran to catch up with her friends. She wondered if there was such a thing as a career in matchmaking.

When Cat got home, she dropped her books on the foyer table. Something there caught her eye. She blinked and looked again. It was a plain white envelope with her name and address. She snatched it up and ran to her room.

Tearing open the envelope, she pulled out the white sheet of paper and sat down on her bed.

Dear Cat,

At night I dream of you, and all day long you never leave my thoughts. I see your beautiful face, I hear your sweet voice, I smell your perfume. I even feel you in my arms. But you're only a vision. Will our love ever become a reality?

I don't know how much longer I can continue to worship you from afar. The pain in my heart is becoming unbearable. Somehow, some way, we must meet. I hope you feel the same. For I know you are my one and only, now and forever love.

Cat fell back on her bed. For a moment she lay perfectly still, enjoying the warm, glowing sensation that surrounded her. Then she jumped up and ran to the phone in Annie and Ben's room.

Just as she was about to grab it, the phone rang. "Hello?"

"Cat, it's me," Marla announced. "Listen to this."

"No, you listen first," Cat said. "I got another letter." She read it over the phone.

She was gratified by Marla's shriek. "It sounds like he's desperate! Oh, Cat, this is so incredible!"

"No kidding. Marla, I've just got to get to Dream Burger again. If he's there and he sees me, maybe he'll get up the nerve to speak. What's *your* news?"

"I don't know any details," Marla reported, "but rumor has it that Heather's bringing a high school boy to the dance."

"A high school boy!" Cat gasped. "So that's why she's been looking so happy."

"At least now you know she's not after Todd," Marla said.

After she hung up, Cat stood there for a moment and considered the news. She supposed it was reassuring to know that Heather didn't have any rotten scheme in mind to get Todd back. But the thought of Heather walking into a junior high dance with a high school boy annoyed her.

Especially since she knew there was a high school boy madly in love with *her*.

One thing Becka especially liked about Mademoiselle Casalls was that she always had tests graded the day after they were given. Tuesday was no exception. As the teacher began distributing the tests at the end of class, Becka waited anxiously. She wasn't actually worried for herself. She was thinking about Keith.

The teacher was taking her time, murmuring words of praise or encouragement to each student, so Becka had the opportunity to develop a real fantasy. Keith wouldn't get a D or an F this time. He'd get a C, maybe even a B minus. He'd be so happy and so grateful to Becka for her help that, in a burst of appreciation, he'd ask her to the dance.

"Becka." The teacher's voice broke through her daydream. She was smiling. "Excellent, as usual."

"Thank you," Becka said, accepting her test, which had a big red A on the front.

She didn't dare turn around, but she strained to listen as Mademoiselle Casalls moved to the desk behind her. She hoped to hear something like "Good, Keith" or "Much better." But she heard nothing.

The teacher returned to the front of the room and the bell rang. Becka whirled around in her seat. "How did you do?" she asked eagerly. As soon as the words flew out of her mouth, she regretted them. What if he had blown it again?

But she needn't have worried. Keith held up the test so she could see the grade.

Becka gasped. "An A?"

Keith grinned as he stuck the papers in his notebook and rose. Becka got up, too, feeling just a little dizzy.

"Wait till I show this to Coach Meadows," Keith said. "Pretty terrific, huh?"

"Terrific," Becka echoed automatically. But her mind was reeling. An A? Keith Doyle got an A in French? No wonder Mademoiselle Casalls was studying him with a skeptical expression as he and Becka moved with the rest of the class toward the door. Just as they reached it, her voice was heard over the hum of conversation. "Keith? Would you remain behind a moment? I'd like a word with you. And Becka, you too, please."

Stiffly, Becka followed Keith back to the teacher's desk. As soon as the last student had left the room, she spoke. "Keith, I was rather amazed by your sudden improvement. And coming so soon after you changed your seat. Can you explain this?"

Keith smiled easily. "Becka's been helping me. She's been giving me tutoring sessions."

Just one session, Becka thought. And not a very

productive one. But when Mademoiselle Casalls asked, "Is this true, Becka?" all she replied was, "*Oui*, mademoiselle."

The teacher nodded, but her eyes seemed to pierce Becka's thoughts, and Becka shivered. Then Mademoiselle Casalls turned her gaze to Keith and her eyes narrowed. "I see. That will be all, for now."

Keith walked ahead of Becka to the door. By the time Becka came out into the hall, he had disappeared. She slowly walked to her next class and tried very hard to push the suspicions out of her mind. Maybe he'd just studied very, very hard. Maybe he'd decided to take his schoolwork seriously. But the rumors Josie had reported to her about Keith kept coming back to her.

Stop it, she scolded herself. *You're jumping to conclusions. You don't know what's going on. You've got absolutely no evidence whatsoever.*

But an *A?* . . .

Josie slammed her locker door shut and looked at the locker across the hall. Where *was* Red, anyway? He always went by his locker after the last class. For once, she didn't have basketball practice, and she wanted to go riding.

Finally, she spotted him coming down the hall. "Red!" she called.

He looked up. For a second his mouth started to form his usual slow, easy grin. But then it turned into something that looked more like a nervous twitch.

"You want to go riding today?" Josie asked him.

"Today?"

"Yeah, today. In about an hour."

He shifted his books from one arm to the other. His face started to redden. "I don't know. Maybe. We could, but . . ." His voice trailed off.

"Look," Josie said impatiently, "either you want to go riding or you don't."

"Um, I've got a lot of homework."

"Oh. Okay." Josie started to turn away.

"Wait," Red said. "If, I mean, if you really want to, I don't know . . ." He was starting to stammer.

"Red! What's the matter with you?"

Now his face was flaming. "Nothing."

Josie was perplexed. "Well, I'm going home. If you want to ride later, call me."

He didn't meet her eyes, but he nodded and went to his locker. He got his coat, closed the door, and walked away.

Josie was still staring after him in bewilderment when Cat came by. "Earth to Josie. Come in, Josie."

"Oh. Hi."

"What's up?"

"It's Red. I wonder if he's feeling all right. He's acting so weird."

"How do you mean, weird?"

Josie tried to explain. "I don't know. All nervous and flustered or something."

Cat laughed gaily. "Josie, that's normal! That's the way guys act when they're in love!"

Josie was about to give her usual response to that suggestion—a groan, a roll of the eyes, and an order to cut it out. But for some reason, Cat's remark didn't trigger that reaction. She looked at her sister uncertainly.

Cat patted her shoulder. "Don't freak out. Just let it happen! You'll see, Josie." Her eyes glazed over. "Being in love . . . it's incredible." She floated away down the hall.

Now Cat was the object of Josie's curious scrutiny. She'd never talked like that about Todd before.

"Are you going straight home?" asked Becka, who had just walked up. When Josie nodded, she said, "Tell Annie and Ben I've got a *Green Gazette* meeting."

"Today? I thought you had meetings on Mondays."

"There must be something special going on. I found a note from Jason on my locker." She didn't sound particularly enthralled with the notion. Her expression was listless.

Jason Wister came tearing up the hall. "Becka, are you coming to the meeting?"

"Yeah. What's the big deal, anyway?"

Jason's face was flushed with excitement. "I've got big news. Dr. Potter called me to his office this afternoon. He read the editorial in the *Gazette*. You know, the one about how we need an honor code."

"That's good," Josie said. "It's nice to know the

89

principal actually pays some attention to what students think.''

"And he liked it!" Jason continued. "He said he thinks there's more cheating going on than he suspected. And he's going to form a committee to look into writing up a policy."

Josie punched him on the shoulder. "The power of the press! Good going! Becka, isn't that great?"

"Yeah," Becka said. "Great." But her voice was flat.

Jason didn't pick up on it. He grabbed Becka's arm. "Come on, I can't be late for my own meeting." Becka allowed herself to be dragged away.

Now Josie had a third person to wonder about. What was the matter with everyone, anyway? Shaking her head, she headed to the exit. Whatever it was, she hoped it wasn't contagious.

Seven

"No basketball practice for two afternoons," Todd told Cat as they strolled down Main Street that afternoon. "I feel like I'm on vacation. I mean, I'm sorry Coach Meadows has the flu, but it's great having some free time for a change."

"Yeah, great," Cat said, only half listening.

"Some of the kids want to go bowling tomorrow after school," Todd went on. "Want to come?"

"Sure."

"By the way, I told Alex we'd double with him and Sharon Saturday night."

"What's Saturday night?"

"The dance!"

"Oh yeah, right." How could she have forgotten? Maybe because she had other things on her mind.

"Is that okay with you?" Todd asked.

"Is what okay?"

"Doubling with Alex and Sharon! Hey, what's the matter with you? You're a regular space cadet."

"It's nothing," Cat said. "Yeah, doubling's fine." But there wasn't much enthusiasm in her voice. When Todd and Alex got together, they acted like clowns.

"You hungry?" Todd asked.

Cat shrugged. Todd took that for a yes. "Let's go to Luigi's."

"Wait," Cat said suddenly. "Not Luigi's. You know, I've got this major craving for a hamburger."

Todd considered this. "We could go to the coffee shop."

"Dream Burger has much better hamburgers," Cat said.

"Dream Burger!" Todd gazed at her in amazement. "What do you want to go there for?"

"Like I said, they've got good hamburgers."

"But we don't hang out at Dream Burger," Todd said.

"We don't have to hang out there," Cat argued. "We'll just have a hamburger and leave."

Todd shook his head. "That's a high school place, Cat. We're not exactly welcome there."

"I don't see any sign on the door that says no junior high students allowed," Cat retorted. "Come on, Todd. It's a free country. We can eat anywhere we want."

Todd glanced at the entrance to Dream Burger as if he actually expected to see a sign proclaiming

No Junior High Students. "I don't think that's a great idea."

"Please," Cat wheedled. "I've been there before and nobody hassled me."

"With who?"

"Marla and her sister Chris."

"That's different," Todd said. "Chris is in high school."

Cat pouted. "Honestly, Todd. I never thought you were the kind of person who would be afraid to go into a place just because a lot of high school kids are there."

"I never said I was *afraid*," Todd replied. He looked at the restaurant again. Reluctance was clearly displayed all over his face. But Cat knew he'd give in. He always did.

"Okay," he said finally. "But let's not stay too long."

"That's fine," Cat agreed. Hopefully, she wouldn't need long. All she wanted was a chance to look around and enough time to be seen.

Of course, there wasn't much she could do there with Todd by her side. But if *he* was there and they made eye contact, at least she could put a face on her daydreams.

Dream Burger was noisy and crowded. There were no empty booths, so Cat and Todd took seats at the counter. Todd's expression was uneasy as he drummed his fingers on the countertop. Looking at him, Cat marveled at the difference a setting could make in a person. At school, Todd was cool and confident. Here, he seemed to shrivel. He looked just as out of place as he had in the French restaurant.

Cat swiveled around on her stool, and her eyes swept the room. Compared to the guys in here, Todd looked almost geeky. And there were lots of guys to compare him to. Tall ones, short ones, light-haired guys, dark-haired guys . . . She had no idea if one was her secret admirer. He might not be here at all, she warned herself. But then again, he might.

She thought she saw one or two guys glance her way. But there was no look of recognition in anyone's eyes.

"Hey, what do you have to do to get some service in here," Todd grumbled.

The guy sitting on his other side turned slightly. "Maybe you got to be a couple of years older."

Todd looked at him sharply. "What did you say?"

The guy sneered. "You heard me, kid."

"Let me hear you say it again."

Cat grabbed his arm. "Todd," she whispered, "don't start anything."

Todd pushed her hand off. The other guy gave a snide laugh. "Hey, that's a hot babe you got there. She deserves better."

With alarm, Cat watched Todd get up. "Want to talk about this outside?"

"Sure. Me and my buddies would enjoy that." With that, two more guys at the counter turned toward Todd with grins that weren't exactly friendly.

"Todd, let's get out of here," Cat said urgently. When he didn't move, she put more emphasis into her words. "Todd! *Please*!"

He grabbed her arm and pulled her toward the door. Behind them, she could hear the guys at the counter laughing.

"They're just a bunch of jerks," Cat said when they got outside.

She'd never seen Todd look so angry. "See? Now are you satisfied?"

Cat was startled by his tone. "It's not my fault you almost got into a fight!"

"I told you I didn't want to go in that place!"

"Why are you making such a big deal about it?" Cat asked.

Todd started walking rapidly. Cat had to run a few steps to catch up with him. Then he stopped and looked at her. "You know, Cat, sometimes I get the feeling you're taking advantage of me."

Cat wasn't sure how to react to that. She took a chance and tried an injured, hurt expression. "Todd. How can you say that?" She reached out and stroked his arm.

For the first time ever, that little gesture didn't bring a smile. She decided to try another tactic. Gazing up at him seriously, she said, "Todd, I simply don't understand what you're talking about. Exactly what do you mean?"

She knew he wouldn't be able to elaborate. Todd wasn't very good at expressing himself. He made a stab at it, though. "It's like . . . sometimes I think you just use me."

"For what?"

"I don't know." Now he was definitely uncomfortable. "Forget it. I've got to get home."

They walked along, side by side. Every now and then, Cat stole a look at his face. But it told her nothing.

At lunch the next day, Josie listened carefully as the boys discussed the condition of the basketball team. Since Alex, Dave, and Jake had all played the year before, they had something to compare this year's team with.

"I'm not worried," Alex said. "Todd's got the speed, even if he can't shoot."

Jake frowned. "Yeah, but if Todd hurts his knee again, we're going to be in trouble. I still wish we had one more forward who could really move."

"Well, we might get one," Dave said. "I think Coach Meadows is going to put Keith Doyle back on the team."

"You're kidding!" Jake exclaimed. "You mean, he's actually getting decent grades?"

"It's amazing, right?" Dave chuckled. "Leave it to Keith to work out a system."

"What kind of system?" Josie asked.

"You should know," Alex said. "Your sister's part of it."

"Becka?" Josie was confused. "You mean, he's got people tutoring him?"

Dave laughed ruefully. "No, he's got people letting him copy their work."

It took a moment for the implication of his statement to sink in. "Are you saying Becka's letting him cheat off her?"

"How do you think he got an A on that French test?" Alex asked.

Josie remembered Becka telling Cat that Keith had moved to the seat behind her. So this was the result of Becka's stupid crush. For a while, she actually thought Becka was becoming less of a wimp. Obviously, she was wrong.

Well, it wasn't *her* problem. Still, she found herself taking quick glimpses across the room to where Becka was sitting with her friends. Abruptly, she rose. "Excuse me," she muttered, and marched across the cafeteria.

"I have to talk to you," Josie said.

Becka looked a little surprised by her tone. "Have a seat."

"Not here," Josie said. "Privately." When Patty and Lisa raised their eyebrows, she added, "No offense." Turning back to Becka, she said, "Meet me in the rest room outside the gym." She knew that at lunchtime it was deserted.

Without giving Becka a chance to protest, she whirled around and headed for the door. She didn't turn to make sure Becka was following her. If Becka was back to being that big a wimp, she'd follow Josie's orders without question.

When she reached the rest room, she did turn, but there was no sign of Becka yet. She was probably apologizing to Patty and Lisa for Josie's rudeness. Josie went inside and paced the area by the sinks and mirrors.

Why did she care what Becka did? Then the answer hit her. Becka was a Morgan. And Josie hated the thought of any Morgan girl letting some sleazy playboy cheat off her just because she wanted a date. It was too sickening for words.

Finally, the rest room door opened and Becka came in. But she wasn't alone. Cat, her eyes bright with curiosity, followed her.

"What are *you* doing here?" Josie demanded, although she had a hunch. Becka must have figured out what Josie had discovered, and she'd brought along Cat for support. Becka never could fight a battle on her own. And Cat was so boy crazy, she'd probably approve of Becka's stupidity.

"Becka said you were excited about something," Cat replied. "What happened? Did Red ask you to go to the dance?"

"This is a lot more important than any dumb dance," Josie said. She fixed Becka with the look she knew made Becka cringe. "Don't you have any pride at all?"

Becka's face was all innocence and bewilderment. "What are you talking about?"

98

"Don't give me that," Josie snapped. "You let Keith Doyle copy the answers from your French test. And don't even try to deny it. He's been bragging about it to the guys."

"Is that all?" Cat rolled her eyes. "You're acting like Becka committed a crime or something."

"She practically did!" Josie stated. "Cheating is wrong. Even you know that."

"But Becka didn't cheat," Cat protested.

"Oh yes she did," Josie retorted. "Didn't you read that article in the newspaper? It said that if one person allows another to cheat, the first person is just as much at fault. If we really had an honor code, Becka would be just as guilty as Keith."

Cat brushed her words away. "That's ridiculous. We don't even have an honor code."

"It's still wrong," Josie insisted.

Cat gave her a withering look. "Josie, when will you ever learn that sometimes you have to do things to get a boy's attention?"

Josie's voice rose. "But he's just using her! And she's letting him! She's being a colossal wimp!"

"Both of you, shut up!"

Josie and Cat jumped at the unfamiliar energy in Becka's voice. Josie was particularly unnerved by Becka's reaction. She'd assumed Becka would whimper, cry even, or at least look extremely upset. She certainly hadn't expected an expression of fierce determination.

When Becka spoke again, her tone was steady.

99

"First of all, I didn't *let* Keith cheat. I didn't know he was copying my answers. And second . . ." She paused and took a deep breath. "I am *not* a wimp!"

There was a moment of silence. "Okay," Josie said. "I believe you didn't know he was cheating. But he's going to keep right on doing it. You better tell the teacher."

"Are you nuts?" Cat asked. To Becka, she said, "You just go right on pretending you don't know what he's doing."

Becka looked at Cat. She looked at Josie. Then she went to the mirror and pulled out a hairbrush from her bag.

"Well, what's it going to be?" Josie demanded.

"Listen to *me*," Cat urged. "I'm the one who wants to help you."

Becka pulled the brush through her hair. Then she turned to Cat. "Yeah, I know. But this time I don't need your help." Her eyes shifted to Josie. "Or yours." She tossed the hairbrush back into her bag and went to the door. She opened it and paused for one last comment. "I can take care of myself, believe it or not."

Cat didn't believe it. "Now you've got her all confused," she accused Josie once Becka had gone. "Why don't you just mind your own business?" She stalked out of the rest room before Josie could respond.

I really shouldn't blame Josie, Cat thought as she walked back to the cafeteria. Josie didn't *have* any of her own business to mind. How could Cat expect

Josie to understand what a girl would do for love when she'd never been in love?

A plan for Josie began to form in her mind. Deep in thought, she didn't see Todd until he was right in front of her. "Hey, I gotta tell you something," he said.

Cat looked up vaguely. "What?"

Todd's eyes seemed to be focused on a point past her. "Um, it's about this afternoon."

"What about this afternoon?" Cat asked with just a hint of impatience. Now that she'd had this bright idea, she wanted to put it into action. Her eyes roamed the cafeteria.

"I know I said we'd go bowling. But something's come up, and—"

"Oh, that's okay," Cat said quickly. She didn't much like bowling anyway. Then she spotted the person she was looking for. "I'll see you later," she told Todd and hurried away.

"Red! Wait a minute. I need to talk to you."

He paused. "I have to get to class."

"I'll walk with you," Cat said. She matched her footsteps with his long stride. "It's about the dance. You know, Saturday night. I think you should ask Josie to go with you. She really wants to go, and she wants to go with *you*. I know you think you guys are just buddies, but she's feeling something else about you. Now, if she knew I was telling you this, she'd kill me." She realized she was chattering and hadn't allowed Red to get a word in. But Red hadn't even tried. In fact, he looked speechless.

"So call her, okay?" Cat asked. "Tonight." Without waiting for a reply, she ran off.

Becka clutched her books tightly as she waited by Keith's locker after the last bell. She needed something to hold on to. Automatically, her eyes lit on the poster hanging on the wall. She wished she didn't want to go to the dance so much. In her mind, she saw herself walking in with Keith, arm in arm. She could see the admiring looks of her classmates. She heard the music. She had the feeling Keith was a good dancer. It was something about the way he moved. There was a swagger to his walk. She saw it now as he came toward her.

"Hi," he said, punctuating his greeting with that incredible smile.

Becka steeled herself. *Why* did he have to look so good? This wasn't going to be easy. "Hi. I wanted to ask you something."

He twirled the combination on his lock. "Ask me no questions, I'll tell you no lies." He winked. "Just kidding. What's up?"

"It's about the French test."

"What about it?"

Becka forced the words out. "Did you . . . did you copy my answers?"

She was watching his hands. They didn't falter as

he finished dialing his combination and opened the locker door. When he spoke, his tone was casual.

"I talked to Coach Meadows. He said if I can keep making grades like that, he's letting me back on the team." He pulled out a sweater. "Test grades aren't going to be enough though. There's homework, too. That's fifty percent of the grade, right?"

"Right," Becka replied softly.

"Maybe I could take a look at yours."

Becka tried to swallow, but the lump in her throat made it too painful. "You want to start copying my homework." It was a statement, not a question.

"I'll change a few answers so Casalls won't catch on," Keith assured her. "Actually, I should have done that on the test. Old Frenchy was suspicious."

At least he wasn't a liar, Becka thought dully. Suddenly, she couldn't bear to look at him. Her eyes went back to the poster.

When she didn't say anything, Keith turned toward her. His eyes followed hers. "Got a date for the dance?"

"No."

"Want one?"

Becka forced herself to face him. "You want to take me to the dance?"

"Sure. I mean, after all you've done for me . . ."

"You don't need to do me any favors," Becka said.

"I don't mind."

"But I do." Becka could feel her face getting hot.

At least she knew she wasn't going to cry. She was too mad to cry. "Besides," she continued, "you don't owe me anything. See, you're not going to be copying my homework. And if you don't change your seat tomorrow, I'll be changing mine."

Despite her anger, she almost enjoyed the stunned look on Keith's face. She didn't allow herself to enjoy it for long. But she knew it was still there as she turned her back on him and walked away.

Eight

For once, Cat could understand why people liked doing good deeds for other people. She was feeling almost saintly as she walked home from school. What a good sister she was! She knew her suggestion to Red had made an impact. He'd ask Josie to the dance, they'd realize they were really in love, and Josie would start behaving like a normal girl. As for Becka, Cat felt sure she'd take her advice about Keith and not Josie's. After all, Becka had always looked up to Cat. Now Becka could have a date for the dance, too.

She recalled a Sunday school teacher back at Willoughby Hall who had told the orphans that a person who did nice things for other people was always rewarded. If that was true, Cat was due for something wonderful very soon.

"Hi," she called out as she entered Morgan's

Country Foods. Annie looked up from the counter where she was ringing up purchases.

"Hi, honey. Have a good day?"

"Very good," Cat replied.

Annie gave the customer his change and beckoned for Cat to come closer. "I think your day's about to become even better. Something arrived for you at home."

"What?"

"Go look. It's on the table in the foyer."

Cat ran out of the store and across the street. Entering the house, her eyes darted to the little table. Then she gasped.

Sitting there was a huge bouquet of flowers. They weren't just regular flowers from someone's garden, either. They were all arranged with bows and wrapped in cellophane. A little envelope stapled to the paper displayed the name of a florist. Scrawled across the envelope was the name Catherine Morgan.

For a moment, Cat just stood there, frozen in a state of ecstasy. No one had ever sent her flowers before. When she recovered from her shock, she carefully pulled the envelope off the cellophane. Her hands were trembling as she removed the card.

The message was brief and to the point. "We must meet. Tonight, ten o'clock, Escapade. Your one and only, now and forever love."

She read it twice to make sure she wasn't seeing things. Clutching the card to her heart, she closed her

106

eyes and let out a sigh of enormous satisfaction. So the Sunday school teacher was right.

She opened her eyes when she heard the front door open. "Wow," Becka exclaimed, taking in the bouquet. "Whose are those?"

"Mine! And guess who they're from?"

Becka's eyes widened. "Your secret admirer?"

Cat nodded happily. "And guess what he wrote on the card?" Before she could go on, the door flew open again and Josie entered. "Nice flowers," she said.

"They're for Cat," Becka told her.

Josie gaped. "Todd sent you flowers?"

"No." Cat shoved the card in her pocket. "They're from someone else."

"I didn't think Todd was that goofy," Josie commented. "Who sent them? They must have cost a fortune."

Cat avoided the question. "Well, boys do crazy things."

"Yeah," Becka sighed. "Really dumb things, too."

"Are you talking about Keith?" Josie asked.

Becka nodded.

Cat frowned. "You mean he still hasn't asked you to the dance?"

Becka studied the floor. "Oh, he asked me."

"Becka!" Cat turned to Josie in triumph. "See? I told you!"

But Becka's next words came as a shock. "I said

no. It was just a bribe. He only asked me so I'd let him copy my homework and cheat off my tests."

Now it was Josie's turn to be triumphant. "And you wouldn't let him. That's super, Becka. I never knew you were that gutsy."

"You call it gutsy," Cat murmured. "I call it stupid."

"No boy's worth getting into trouble for," Becka said. "Or doing something you know is wrong."

Cat could only shake her head sadly. She hadn't expected Becka to be such a goody-goody. Thank goodness she hadn't shown her the card from the flowers. Gathering them in her arms, she swept past the others and went up to her room.

There, she had a chance to look at the card again and think. Escapade. That was the club she'd heard about, the one that was letting in underage kids. It was on Green Street, she remembered. And he wanted her to be there at ten o'clock.

This was going to take some planning. She considered the possibilities. Then she got up and walked out of the room. She could hear Josie and Becka downstairs, talking. She hurried into Annie and Ben's room, shut the door, and went to the phone.

"Marla, it's Cat. Wait till you hear this. *He* wants to meet me tonight at Escapade."

The screech on the other end was extremely satisfying. But Cat didn't even give it time to die down before she continued. "I need your help." Speaking rapidly, she told Marla what she wanted her to do.

Then she heard footsteps on the stairs. "I have to go," she said in a rush. "Thanks!"

Opening the door, she practically collided with Annie. Annie seemed startled at finding her in their bedroom with the door closed. "I—I had to talk to Marla about something private."

Annie's eyes twinkled. "Telling her about the flowers?"

"Exactly," Cat said, glad she didn't have to make up a major lie. She started down the stairs.

"Who were the flowers from?" Annie called after her.

Cat laughed lightly. "Just some silly boy at school. He's got a crush on me."

"You mean Todd's got competition?"

"Looks like it!"

They were all just sitting down to dinner when the phone rang. Cat leaped up. "I'll get it!" She tore into the kitchen. "Hello?"

"Uh, hi, it's Red. Can I speak to Josie?"

"Hang on." She went back to the dining room. "Josie, it's for you. Red."

"Tell him I'll call him back after dinner."

"You tell him," Cat said.

Sighing, Josie rose and went into the kitchen.

"Cat got flowers today," Annie told Ben as she passed him a bowl of beef stew.

"Flowers!" Ben exclaimed. "From whom?"

"Just a boy," Cat said.

Ben shook his head in amazement. "Thirteen-year-

109

old boys must be a lot more romantic than they were in my day," he mused.

Cat tried to picture Todd—or any other boy at school—sending her flowers. Not very likely.

"Boys must have a lot more money, too," Annie added. "It's a huge bouquet."

Both Annie and Ben were looking at Cat with curious interest. Cat plunged her spoon into the stew. "This is delicious."

Josie returned, and she looked disturbed. This drew Annie and Ben's attention away from Cat. "Is something the matter with Red?" Annie asked.

"Yeah." Josie sat down. "He just asked me to the dance."

Cat clapped her hands. "See? I was right again! Red *is* in love with you!"

Ben almost choked on his stew. "What?"

Annie was startled, too. "Josie! I had no idea. I thought you and Red were just good friends."

"That's what I thought, too," Josie said glumly.

"It's strange," Becka murmured. "You think a guy is one way and he turns out to be another."

"I think this is fabulous," Cat stated firmly. "Are you going to get a new dress? You should have a manicure, too, and—"

"Hold on," Josie interrupted. "I haven't even told him whether or not I'll go. I said I'd have to think about it."

"But you *have* to go!" Cat exclaimed. "You can't

110

hurt his feelings. Here he's finally gotten up the courage to ask you out. If you turn him down, it could absolutely destroy him!"

"Now, Cat," Ben said, "I wouldn't go that far. I've been turned down by a girl or two in my time, and I survived."

"Red might be more sensitive," Cat argued.

"Josie certainly doesn't have to go on a date with Red if she doesn't want to go out with him," Annie noted.

"I like being with Red," Josie said. "But why do we have to go on a *date*? And I hate dances."

"You've never even been to one," Cat pointed out.

"Yeah, but wearing a dress, dancing . . . yuck."

The phone rang again. Ben started to rise, but Cat got up first. "Hello?"

"Hi, it's Marla. Here's your call."

Cat waited a few seconds. Then, loudly, she said, "I'll have to ask and see if it's okay. I'll call you back."

In the dining room, she announced, "That was Marla. She wants me to come over tonight to work on this project we have for pep club."

"Tonight?" Ben frowned. "What about your homework?"

"I did most of it in study hall," Cat fibbed. "And I can finish what's left before I go."

"But it's a weeknight," Annie said. "Can't you and Marla work on this project after school?"

111

"Marla baby-sits after school every day," Cat explained. To support her case, she added another lie. "And we, um, can't work this weekend because . . . because we have to have it done by Friday." Strange, how she was stumbling over her words. Lies usually came so easily to her.

She could feel Becka and Josie looking at her skeptically. It was very hard to meet Annie's eyes, or Ben's. "It's really important. And I'll be in trouble with the pep club if we don't get this done." She turned on every ounce of charm she possessed. *"Please?"*

"How is Cat getting home from Marla's?" Annie asked Ben.

"She said Marla's sister would drive her home. But I told her to call and let us know when she was leaving. What time is it?"

Annie looked at her watch. "Almost ten."

Ben's brow furrowed. "She'd better call soon."

"You know how Cat loses track of the time," Becka said.

"What are you defending her for?" Josie grumbled.

"Are you angry at Cat?" Annie asked.

Josie sighed. "No. It's just that she keeps bugging me to go to this dance with Red. I wish she would quit trying to make me and Becka act like her."

Becka smiled. "That's just the way Cat is. Besides, you don't have to listen to her."

"But I don't want to hurt Red's feelings," Josie went on. "I guess it wouldn't kill me to go to one dance." She got up. "I'm going to call him now."

She was just reaching for the phone when it rang. "Hello?"

The voice at the other end was muffled, and Josie could barely make out the words, "Mr. Morgan, please."

"Just a minute. Ben, it's for you," she called out.

Ben joined her in the kitchen and took the phone. "Hello?" There was a pause. *What?*

Josie watched his expression in alarm. Something was wrong.

"Who is this?" Ben demanded. He stared at the receiver, then slowly replaced it.

Annie came in. "Who was that?"

"I don't know. It was a female voice. She asked me if I knew where my daughter was. Then she said Cat is at Escapade."

Annie went pale. "The nightclub?"

"Maybe it was a prank," Josie suggested.

"What's Marla's number?" Ben asked. Annie picked up the Green Falls telephone directory and flipped through it. As she recited the number, Ben dialed it. "Hello, Mrs. Eastman? This is Ben Morgan. Is Cat there?" His face hardened. "I see. Thank you." Hanging up, he turned to Annie. "Cat hasn't been there all evening."

Annie's hand flew to her mouth. Ben strode out of

113

the kitchen, went to the hall closet, and pulled out a jacket. "Exactly where is this Escapade?"

It was chilly outside. Cat hugged her sweater closer. Glancing down at her jeans, she wished she could have worn something a little more spectacular for their first meeting. But Annie and Ben would have become suspicious if she'd dressed up just to go to Marla's.

Nervously, she looked up at the neon sign proclaiming this to be Escapade. There were no windows, so she couldn't see inside. She'd been standing out there for five minutes, and she'd seen several adults go inside. This was definitely not a kids' place. But the older girls had said anyone could get in. And somewhere in that place waited her one and only, now and forever love.

The thought gave her strength. Trying to look like she went into this kind of place every night, she opened the door. A man standing just inside muttered, "Five dollars."

Cat fumbled in her purse and pulled out a bill. The man barely glanced at her as he took it. Cat moved into the main room.

It took a few minutes for her eyes to become accustomed to the darkness. Between the dim lighting and the deafening music, she felt a little dizzy. Once her eyes adjusted, she made out a lot of figures on the dance floor. So many people . . . how was she going to find him? She'd just have to let him find her.

Along one wall was a counter with stools. Cat edged around the dancers and made her way there.

"What'll it be?" a man behind the counter asked.

"Um, a Diet Coke, please." She lifted herself onto one of the stools. The man brought her Coke, and Cat started sipping it. She wasn't thirsty, but it gave her something to do.

She felt so uncomfortable. She wasn't sure if it was this place or what she'd had to do to get there. Funny, telling little white lies had never bothered her before. She used to tell them all the time back at Willoughby Hall, to get out of chores and stuff like that. And she'd told some when she first came to the Morgans', mainly to avoid working at the store. At school, she never had a problem inventing stories.

Why did she feel so creepy about it this time? It was a dumb question. In her heart, she knew. It had something to do with lying to Annie and Ben. Lying to people who trusted her, who loved her.

But it was love that had brought her here, too. She'd had no choice.

Where was he, anyway? It was too dark to read her watch, but it had to be after ten by now. Surely he could see her sitting there. She certainly felt conspicuous enough. She swiveled on her stool to survey the room.

"Cat."

The voice came from behind her. It was unmistakably male. It was also unmistakably familiar. Slowly, she turned. Ben stood there, his arms folded across his chest, his face stern.

Cat had a pretty good suspicion all the charm in the world wouldn't get her out of this one.

Nine

On Saturday evening, Cat sat cross-legged on her bed and for the hundredth time in three days, bemoaned her fate. "Grounded. For two weeks. *Two weeks*!"

Sitting beside her, Becka patted her on the back. "Try to look on the bright side. It could have been for a month."

"And I didn't even meet him," Cat wailed.

"If he really loves you, he'll find a way to meet you," Becka said.

Cat's eyes drifted to the bouquet, which was still sitting on her dresser. The flowers were starting to turn brown and wilt. She hadn't had any more letters.

"What did Todd say when you told him you couldn't go to the dance?" Becka asked.

Cat shrugged. "He didn't say much. He didn't even act all that upset."

Becka nodded. "Boys don't show their feelings like girls do."

"How do you know so much about boys all of a sudden?" Cat asked.

"I'm learning," Becka replied. "Where's Josie?"

"In the bath. Isn't it weird? Of the three of us, she's the only one going to the dance."

Becka grinned. "And she's the only one who doesn't *want* to go."

Cat couldn't help grinning back. Then they both started to giggle.

"What's so funny?" Annie stood in the doorway.

"Josie," Becka said. "Going to a dance."

Annie smiled slightly. "I have to admit, she hasn't been particularly excited about this. Maybe we can all pitch in and get her spirits up." She came in the room. Standing by the girls, she stroked Cat's hair. Cat looked up. There was so much warmth in Annie's eyes. It truly amazed her. Despite what she'd done, Annie and Ben still loved her.

Josie, wrapped in a robe, stomped in. "Well, I'm clean."

"That's a start," Cat said. She got up. "Now, what are we going to do about your hair?"

Josie stepped back. "I'm not letting you stick those hot things on my head again."

"But it's so straight!"

"I like it straight," Josie insisted. "And no makeup, either."

"You're hopeless," Cat grumbled.

118

"What are you going to wear?" Becka asked.

Josie flopped down on her bed. "I haven't even thought about that."

"*I* have," Annie said, and hurried out.

"Cheer up," Becka said to Josie. "It might be fun."

Josie wrinkled her nose. "I doubt it. I still can't figure out why Red wants to go."

Annie reappeared, carrying a bag from Danielle's Boutique, one of the nicest stores in town. She held it out to Josie.

"Oh, wow," Cat breathed as Josie pulled a dress from the bag. It was a deep midnight blue, simple but elegant, with long sleeves and a dropped waist. Josie held it in front of her and turned to the mirror.

"The color's perfect for you," Becka said.

"It brings out your eyes," Annie added.

They all watched while an expressionless Josie examined her reflection. Finally, her face broke into a smile. "I guess if I have to wear a dress, it might as well be a pretty one." She turned and hugged Annie. "Thanks."

Cat watched in envy. She should be the one with the new dress. And it was her own fault she wasn't.

It didn't take Josie long to get ready. Cat was able to talk her into just a little makeup.

"How about some jewelry?" Annie suggested.

Josie wiggled the finger that held her little ruby ring, identical to the ones Becka and Cat wore. Annie and Ben had given them to the girls, to celebrate their becoming a family. "Isn't this enough?"

But Annie insisted on lending her some tiny pearl earrings, and she contributed a spray of her best perfume.

"Darling, you look beautiful," Annie said.

Privately, Cat thought that was an exaggeration, but she had to admit Josie didn't look half-bad. They all went downstairs.

"Who is this gorgeous creature?" Ben cried out as they entered the living room.

"I'm not sure," Josie said. "I certainly don't feel like me. Especially in these shoes." The heels weren't very high, but she was teetering in them. "How am I supposed to dance in these? I can't even dance in flat shoes."

"Well, you're going to have to," Cat said. "That's what you do at dances." She looked at the clock on the mantel. "Where is Red, anyway? The dance started at eight, and it's already quarter after."

"Maybe he's got cold feet," Josie said. "Mine are freezing."

But just then the doorbell rang. On unsteady feet, Josie went to the door. Red stood there. He produced a rather sickly smile for her. And he was unusually awkward as he greeted the others and shook hands with Annie and Ben.

"Are you sure you two don't want a ride over to school?" Ben asked.

"No thanks," Josie said. "We'll walk."

"Hope she makes it," Becka whispered to Cat.

Red turned to Josie. "Ready?"

"Yeah." Her face was as grim as his. Together they walked out.

Cat shook her head. "You'd think they were going to a funeral, not a dance."

"Well, maybe they'll start enjoying themselves once they're there," Annie said, but her tone didn't carry much hope.

The phone rang. For once, Cat didn't jump up to get it. Who'd be calling her when everyone was at the dance? She was startled when Annie called to her from the kitchen.

"Maybe it's *him*," Becka hissed in Cat's ear. Cat ran to the kitchen and picked up the phone. "Hello?"

"Hi, it's me."

"Oh. Hi, Marla. You sound funny."

"I'm calling from the pay phone outside the gym. I can't talk any louder or someone will hear me."

"How's the dance?" Cat asked.

"It's okay. But Heather just walked in. And you're not going to believe who she's with."

"Some high school boy, right?"

"No, that was just a rumor. Cat, maybe you better sit down."

Suddenly, Cat knew what Marla was about to tell her. "Just say it, Marla. She's with Todd, right?"

"Yeah."

Cat stamped her foot. "That creep!" she raged. "Just because I'm grounded, he goes running back to that witch! Oh, I'm never going to speak to him again! Never!"

"I just thought you'd rather hear it from me," Marla whispered into the phone. "It'll be all over school by Monday."

And I'll be the girl who got dumped, Cat thought as she hung up the phone. Her eyes were burning. *Oh, Todd,* she thought. *How could you do this to me?* And did he have to take Heather, his ex-girlfriend and her number-one worst enemy?

It was all so embarrassing and humiliating and totally awful. She grabbed a napkin and wiped her eyes. There was no way she was going to cry over Todd. She'd much rather strangle him. And then a thought occurred to her that *really* made her want to cry. Now she wouldn't even get nominated for homecoming queen!

"You look very nice," Red said in a strained voice.

"So do you," Josie replied. Then they both lapsed into silence. Josie thought about all the time she spent with Red. They usually never stopped talking. Now, as she hobbled along by his side, she couldn't think of a thing to say.

"They're having a live band at this dance," Red said.

"That's nice."

There was another awkward silence. "Have you ever been to a dance before?" Red asked.

"No."

"Then, how come . . . why do you want so much to go to this one?"

Josie stared at him. "Who said I wanted to go to the dance?"

"Cat. She said you'd be really hurt if I didn't ask you."

Josie stopped walking. "Cat told me you'd be really hurt if I told you I didn't want to go."

They stared at each other for a second. Then Red averted his eyes. Josie looked away, too. "Red . . . did Cat tell you I was, uh . . ." She tried to think of a way to say this without sounding too sickening. "That I wanted to be . . . more than your friend?"

Even in the darkness, she could see him blush. "Well, yeah. Sort of."

Josie groaned. "She's been trying to convince me that you're the one who's, um, getting romantic."

They were both finding it impossible to look each other in the eye. Finally, Red asked the question. "Do you?"

"Do I what?"

He practically choked on the words. "Want to be . . . more than friends?"

The answer came easier to Josie. "We already are. You're just about my *best* friend. But I'm not interested in anything like . . . you know."

The relief on his face was clear. "Same here. Do you really want to go to this dance?"

"Not particularly. Do you?"

Red shook his head.

123

"Well, we have to do something," Josie said.

Red brightened. "How about bowling?"

"Bowling? Dressed like this?"

"Why not? There are no rules about clothes, just shoes. And we can get those there."

Josie grinned. "And I'll be able to walk." She linked her arm in his. "Let's go."

They did get a few odd glances in the bowling alley, particularly after Josie changed into bowling shoes. They didn't exactly go with the dress she was wearing. But she didn't care. She concentrated on trying out several balls before selecting the right one.

Red looked a lot more relaxed, too. "Hey, what do you think Cat would say if she knew we ended up here?"

"She'd say we were both very sick," Josie replied.

Red touched his forehead. "I feel pretty good myself. How about you?"

Josie stood in front of the lane and aimed her ball. "I feel fabulous." She rolled the ball. "A strike! I got a strike!" She threw her arms around Red. Then, very quickly, she withdrew them.

But Red was grinning. And he didn't even blush.

Ben came into the living room.

"Who were you talking to on the phone?" Annie asked.

"The mayor. It seems there's been one positive result of Cat's little adventure the other night. It provided evidence that Escapade *has* been letting underage kids in. Now the mayor's got the proof he needs to order the place closed."

"Gee," Cat said. "So I've really done something good for the town."

"In a manner of speaking," Ben agreed. "But don't get the idea that this is going to reduce your sentence."

Cat's face fell. Ben put a gentle hand on her shoulder. "Two weeks isn't that long."

"It's not just that," Cat said. "It's Todd. He took Heather to the dance at school."

"Oh, Cat," Annie murmured. There was real compassion in her voice.

Ben looked sorry, too. "Well, he's a real jerk, then. They talk about women being flighty. Sometimes I think men are worse."

"No kidding," Becka muttered.

"Oh, dear," Annie said. "Have you had a bad experience, too?"

"Yeah." Becka told them about Keith.

When she finished her story, Annie groaned. "Men." She tossed a pillow at Ben.

Ben responded with an injured look. "Hey, don't blame the whole sex for a couple of rotten apples. Believe me, girls, there are a few good guys out there."

"He's right," Annie said. "I found one, didn't I?" She leaned over and planted a kiss on her husband's cheek.

"I think," Ben said slowly, "that our daughters

need a little cheering up. Any ideas as to how we might accomplish that?"

"I only know one sure cure for depression," Annie said. "Chocolate. Unfortunately, there's none in the house."

"Then I say we go in search of some," Ben said. "Come on, girls, we're going to Brownies."

There weren't many people in the restaurant. It was too early for the after-movie crowd. And all the kids their age were at the dance. They settled in a booth and gave their orders to the waitress.

There was a question in Cat's head that had been nagging her. She hadn't wanted to bring it up before. But now seemed the right time. "Ben, how did you know I'd gone to Escapade the other night?"

"I got a phone call."

"Who from?"

"I don't know. It was a female voice, though."

"Cat," Annie said, "you never told us *why* you went there."

Cat started to fabricate a story. But for some reason, she stopped and decided to tell the truth. "A guy asked me to meet him there."

"What guy?" Ben asked.

"I don't know." All of a sudden, she felt a little silly. "I have this . . . this secret admirer. He's been writing to me."

"And he sent her those flowers," Becka piped up. "Isn't it romantic?"

126

"Where did you meet this secret admirer?" Annie asked.

"I haven't actually met him. He saw me at Dream Burger. He wrote that he couldn't get me out of his mind."

"And he called her—what did he call you?" Becka asked.

Cat reddened. "His one and only, now and forever love."

"Good grief," Annie said. She didn't look impressed.

Ben was actually frowning. "Cat, that could have been very dangerous. You don't know anything about this person. He could have been a criminal."

"Oh, no," Cat said. "Everyone at Dream Burger is in high school."

"Even so," Ben began, but Becka suddenly clutched Cat's arm.

"Cat, look."

Cat's stomach turned over. Walking into Brownies were Todd and Heather. They sat down at a table near the entrance.

Annie and Ben saw them, too. Both grimaced.

"That's the girl he picked over you?" Ben asked. "He's dumber than I thought. And I question his eyesight."

Cat smiled sadly. "Thanks." It dawned on her that she didn't have any makeup on, not even lipstick. And just in case they saw her . . . "Excuse me a minute."

In the rest room, she made some repairs to her

face. She was brushing her hair when the door swung open. Heather sauntered in.

"Why, Cat," she said sweetly. "What a surprise. Who are you here with?"

Cat kept her head high. "My parents."

Heather raised her eyebrows. "Your parents? On a Saturday night?" Her lips twitched, as if she was trying to keep from laughing.

"Why aren't you at the dance?" Cat asked.

"It was boring," Heather said airily. "Too many seventh-graders crowding the dance floor. Todd hates crowds, you know." She pulled out a comb and ran it lightly over hair that was already perfect.

Cat stared at her own reflection. *My eyes are so much greener than hers,* she thought fiercely.

"Of course," Heather continued, "if we'd known you were here, we wouldn't have come. It must be so painful for you to see Todd now." She put the comb back in her purse and went to the door. Opening it, she paused and looked back. "But don't be too sad, Cat. I'm sure any day now, you'll find your one and only, now and forever love."

For an instant, Cat froze. Then she whirled around. But Heather was gone. Only her parting words lingered in the air. *Her one and only, now and forever love.* What her secret admirer had called her. How could Heather have known?

Then, like a lightening bolt, it hit her. Suddenly, everything made sense. She knew how the secret admirer had learned her name. She knew why he'd never tell her his. She knew why he didn't show up at Escapade.

There *was* no secret admirer. It was a setup, a prank, Heather's finest scheme so far. She had seen Cat coming out of Dream Burger. She had sent the letters and the flowers. She had made the phone call to Ben.

And Cat had fallen for it all. She turned back to the mirror and faced herself. The strangest assortment of feelings were churning inside her. First, she wanted to cry over the loss of the boy who never even was. Then she wanted to laugh at herself for being such a fool.

But it wasn't long before a stronger emotion took over. Anger. And a burning desire for revenge.

She'd get back at Heather for this. She could always figure out a way to get Todd back. Of course, she wasn't so sure she wanted him back. Maybe she'd have to come up with some other way to make Heather suffer. Something really horrendous. . . .

She didn't know what, or how, or when. But she'd come up with something. Nobody pulled a stunt like this on Cat Morgan and got away scot-free. Heather was going to *pay.*

Thoughts of revenge improved her mood. But she still felt like such a fool. She spoke to her reflection. "Cat, for a smart girl, you can be really stupid."

The rest room door opened and Becka came in. "Hey, are you okay? You've been in here forever."

Cat turned around, and Becka stepped back in alarm. "You look you're ready to kill someone!"

"I am," Cat said grimly. "But don't worry. It's not you. Come on." She started toward the door. "Now I'm in *serious* need of chocolate."

Here's a sneak peek at what's ahead in the exciting fifth book of THREE OF A KIND:
Cat Morgan, Working Girl

Cat walked at a steady pace, her face set in a grim expression. Glancing at her watch, she quickened her step. She knew what Miss Andrews' reaction would be if she was late. This was only her second real working day at the Green Falls Inn. She wished it was her last.

Her thoughts went back to Friday. It had been a disaster. She couldn't do anything right, at least not according to Miss Andrews, the manager. Cat left streaks on the windows, she didn't sweep properly, and she broke one of the stupid china figurines on the lobby mantel while she was dusting. For two hours, Miss Andrews had hovered over her, scolding and snapping and complaining. Well, what did she expect? Cat Morgan was *not* cut out to be a maid.

Somehow, she'd managed to keep up a brave front

at home over the weekend. She couldn't very well let Ben and Annie know how miserable she was, not when she was working for their friends. Even thinking about her new dress from Danielle's Boutique didn't bring much comfort, considering what she was going through to get it.

In her eyes, the Green Falls Inn no longer looked pretty and quaint. It was beginning to resemble a torture chamber. With extreme reluctance, she opened the door and went in.

"Morgan!"

Cat flinched. "Yes, Miss Andrews?"

"What are you waiting for? Get into your uniform immediately."

Cat went into the little bathroom behind the reception desk and took off her skirt and sweater. Then, with a grimace, she slipped into her uniform and tied the apron around her waist. She tried to avoid the mirror, but years of habit forced her eyes automatically in that direction.

For once, she didn't smile and preen at the image she saw. Her reflection revolted her. Gray had to be her very worst color. It made her skin look yellow. The uniform was baggy and shapeless. And that wretched apron! It was like a sign, telling the whole world she was a maid.

Scowling, she pulled her hair back in an elastic band, the way Miss Andrews insisted she wear it. One lock refused to be gathered and fell down the side of her face.

I look like Cinderella, Cat thought. *Before* the visit from her fairy godmother. She could only be grateful that all the guests here were from out of town, and she wasn't likely to ever see any of them again.

Out in the lobby, Miss Andrews' piercing eyes hit Cat. "Follow me." She led Cat to a storage closet, where she took out a can of furniture polish and a nasty-looking rag. "Do the banister."

Cat took the rag gingerly between two fingers and went to the stairs.

Miss Andrews snatched the rag out of her hands. "Like this!" She rubbed the railing vigorously. "Haven't you ever polished furniture before?" She snorted. "Are you afraid of ruining your nails?"

Cat pressed her lips together tightly so the response she was forming in her head wouldn't come out of her mouth. A rush of conflicting emotions battled inside her. On the one hand, she wanted to inform this witch that she had lived in an orphanage for thirteen years and had done her share of drudgery. Not to mention the fact that she had regular chores at home.

"Okay, get to work."

Cat rubbed until the manager left the area. Then she examined her hands. Already, the polish was leaving brown streaks. Gook was collecting under her fingernails. The polish on a nail was chipped. Waves of self-pity engulfed her.

Two women came down the stairs and stepped

past her as if she were invisible. Well, who *would* notice a maid? Oh, the shame of it all. . . .

Step by step, she mounted the stairs, dragging the rag across the banister. Thank goodness, her friends couldn't see her now. Her lunchmates knew she was working here, but she'd managed to avoid telling them exactly what she did. Her reputation would be in shreds.

Finally, Cat reached the top. Then she stepped back down, glancing at the banister as she went. It didn't look any different to her.

Miss Andrews was nowhere in sight. Thankfully, Cat collapsed on the bottom stair. Through the railing, she felt a cold breeze as the door to the Inn opened.

Sally Layton, the owner, said, "Good afternoon. May I help you?"

A woman's voice replied, "Yes, we're meeting the Hudsons for tea. Have they arrived?"

"I'll call their room," Sally said. "Could I have your name, please?"

"Mrs. Beaumont."

Cat froze, then slowly turned her head to get a look. A tall woman with streaked blond hair, wearing a mink coat, stood there. She wasn't alone. Cat swallowed and almost choked. Standing beside Mrs. Beaumont was Heather.